THE CROSSOVER

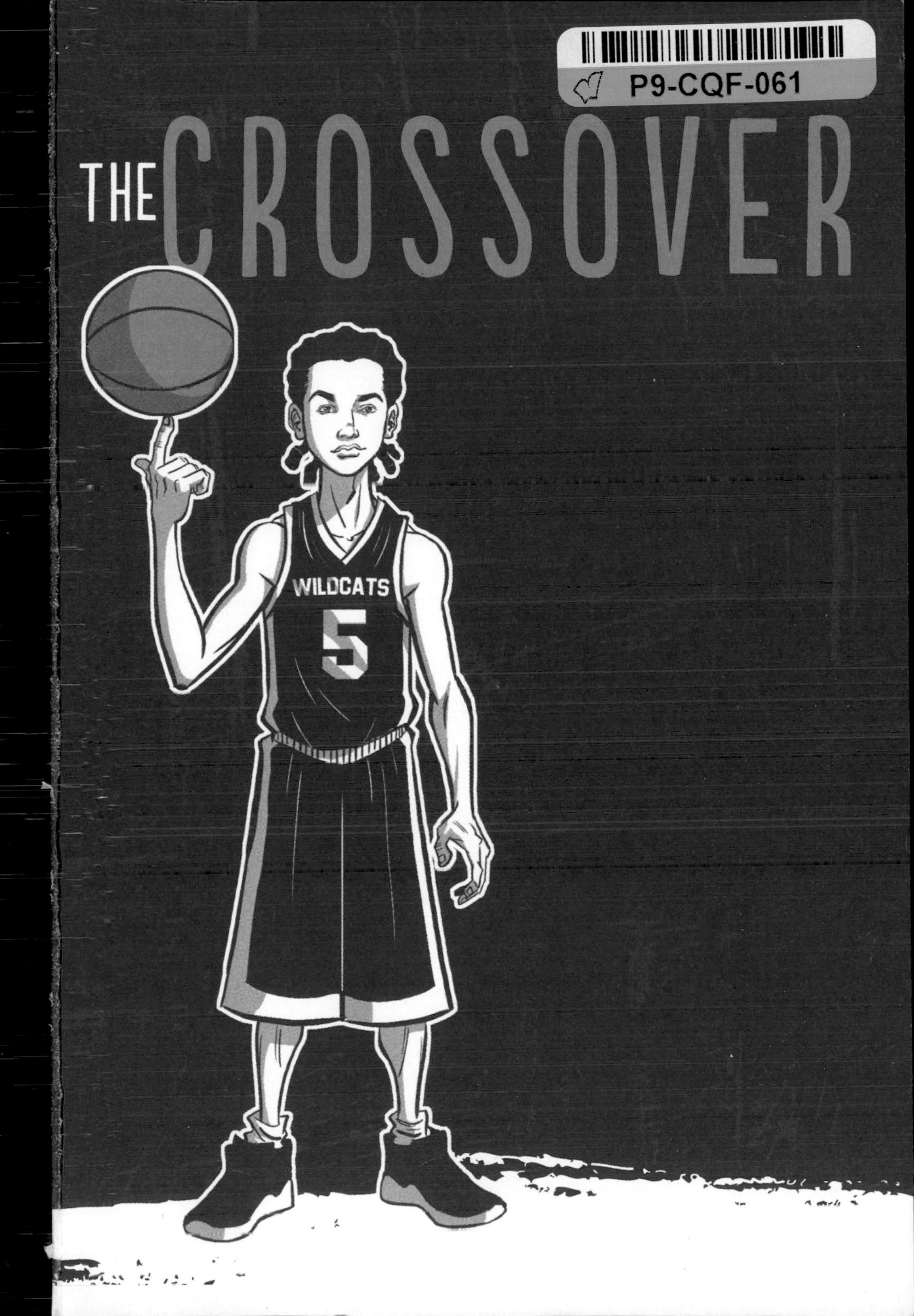
WILDCATS
5

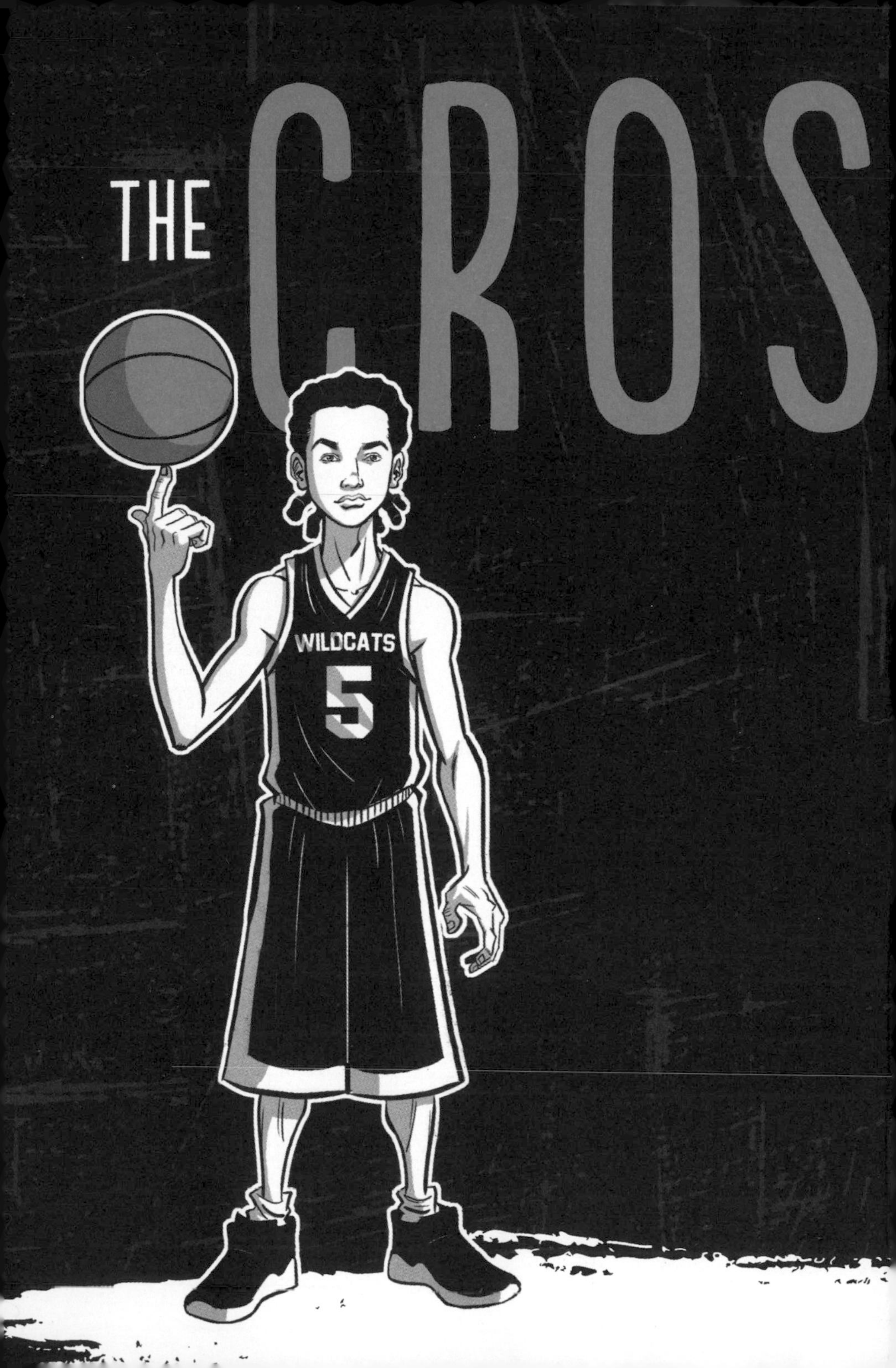
THE CROS
WILDCATS
5

SOVER

BY KWAME ALEXANDER

ILLUSTRATED BY DAWUD ANYABWILE

HOUGHTON MIFFLIN HARCOURT
BOSTON NEW YORK

For Samayah and Jackson-Leroi
—K.A.

I dedicate this book to the memory of my high school art
teacher and mentor, the late Mr. Bernard Harmon—
Central High School of Philadelphia. Thank you for your
guidance, patience, and instruction.
—D.A.

Text copyright © 2014 by Kwame Alexander
Illustrations copyright © 2019 by Dawud Anyabwile

hmhbooks.com

Library of Congress Cataloging-in-Publication Data is on file.

ISBN: 978-1-328-96001-6 (hardcover)
ISBN: 978-1-328-57549-4 (paperback)
ISBN: 978-0-358-16474-6 (signed edition)

Manufactured in China
SCP 10 9 8 7 6 5 4 3 2 1
4500758568

WARM-UP

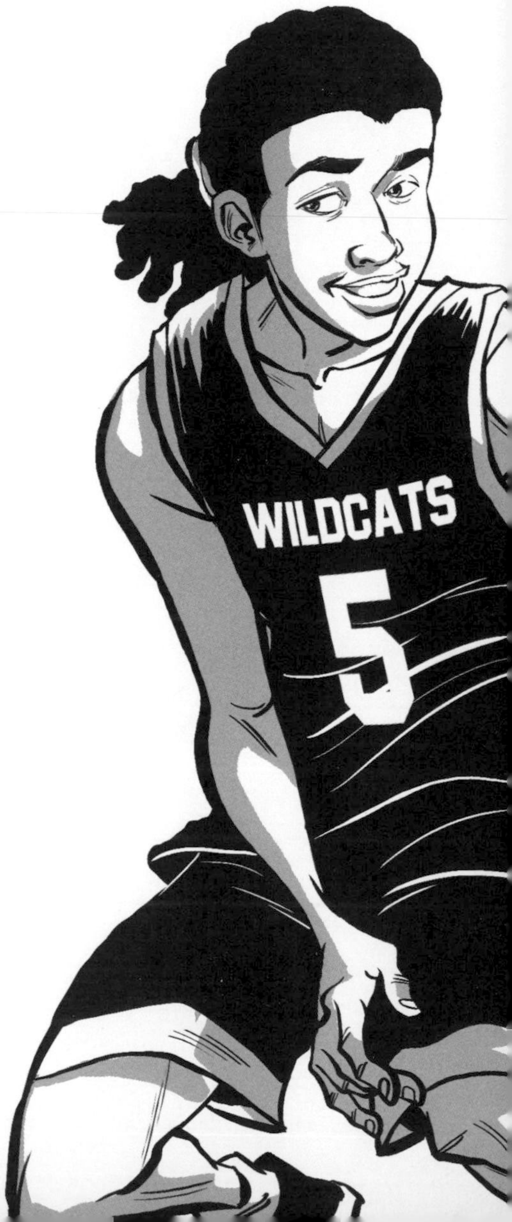
WILDCATS
5

DRIBBLING

AT THE TOP OF THE KEY, I'M
MOVING & GROOVING,
POPPING AND ROCKING —

WHY YOU BUMPING?

WHY YOU LOCKING?
MAN, TAKE THIS THUMPING.

BE CAREFUL THOUGH, 'CAUSE NOW I'M CRUNKING

CRISSCROSSING

FLOSSING

FLIPPING AND MY DIPPING
WILL LEAVE YOU

SLIPPING

ON THE
FLOOR,

WHILE I SWOOP IN TO THE FINISH
WITH A FIERCE FINGER ROLL...
WILDCATS

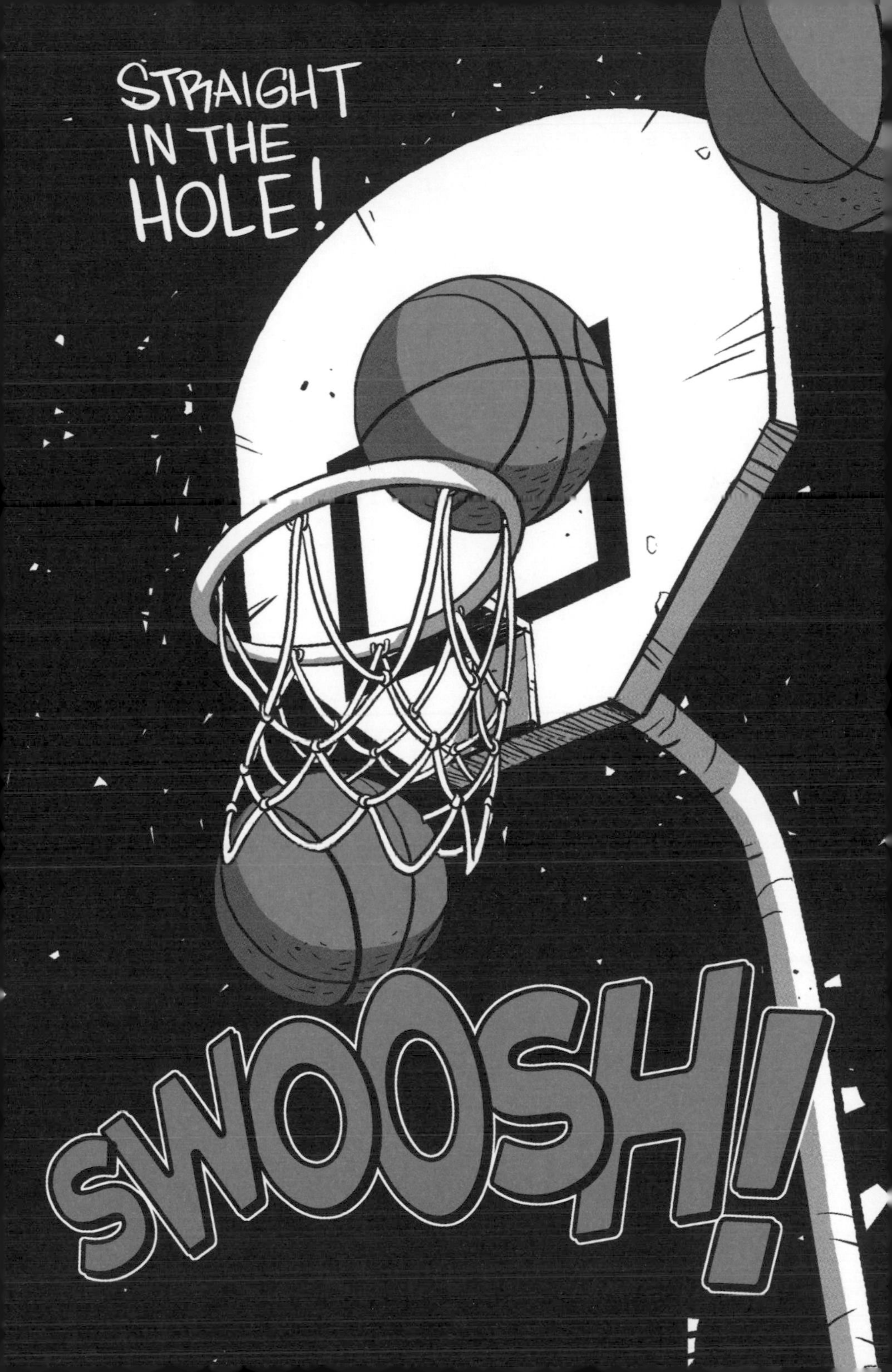
STRAIGHT IN THE HOLE!
SWOOSH!

JOSH BELL IS MY NAME.

BUT FILTHY McNASTY IS MY CLAIM TO FAME.

FOLKS CALL ME THAT 'CAUSE MY GAME'S ACCLAIMED,

SO DOWNRIGHT DIRTY,

IT'LL PUT YOU TO SHAME.

MY HAIR IS LONG,

MY HEIGHT'S TALL.

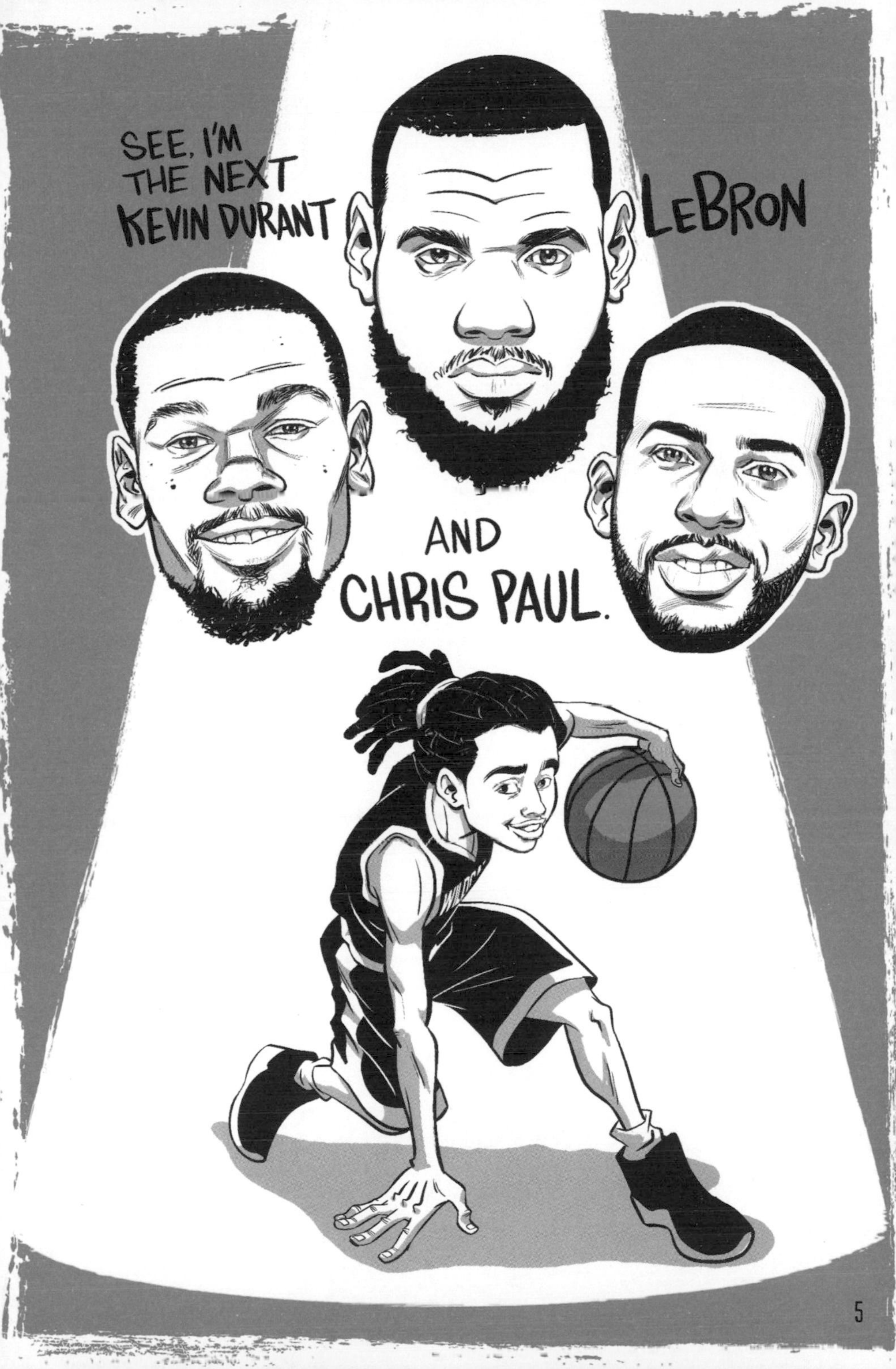
SEE, I'M THE NEXT KEVIN DURANT
LEBRON
AND CHRIS PAUL.

REMEMBER THE **GREATS,** MY DAD LIKES TO **GLOAT:**

I BALLED WITH **MAGIC** AND THE **GOAT.**

BUT TRICKS ARE FOR KIDS, I REPLY.

DON'T NEED YOUR PETS MY GAME'S **SO FLY.**

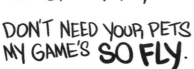

MOM SAYS, YOUR DAD'S OLD SCHOOL, LIKE AN OL' CHEVETTE.

YOU'RE FRESH AND NEW, LIKE A RED CORVETTE.

YOUR GAME SO SWEET,

IT'S A CRÊPES SUZETTE.

7

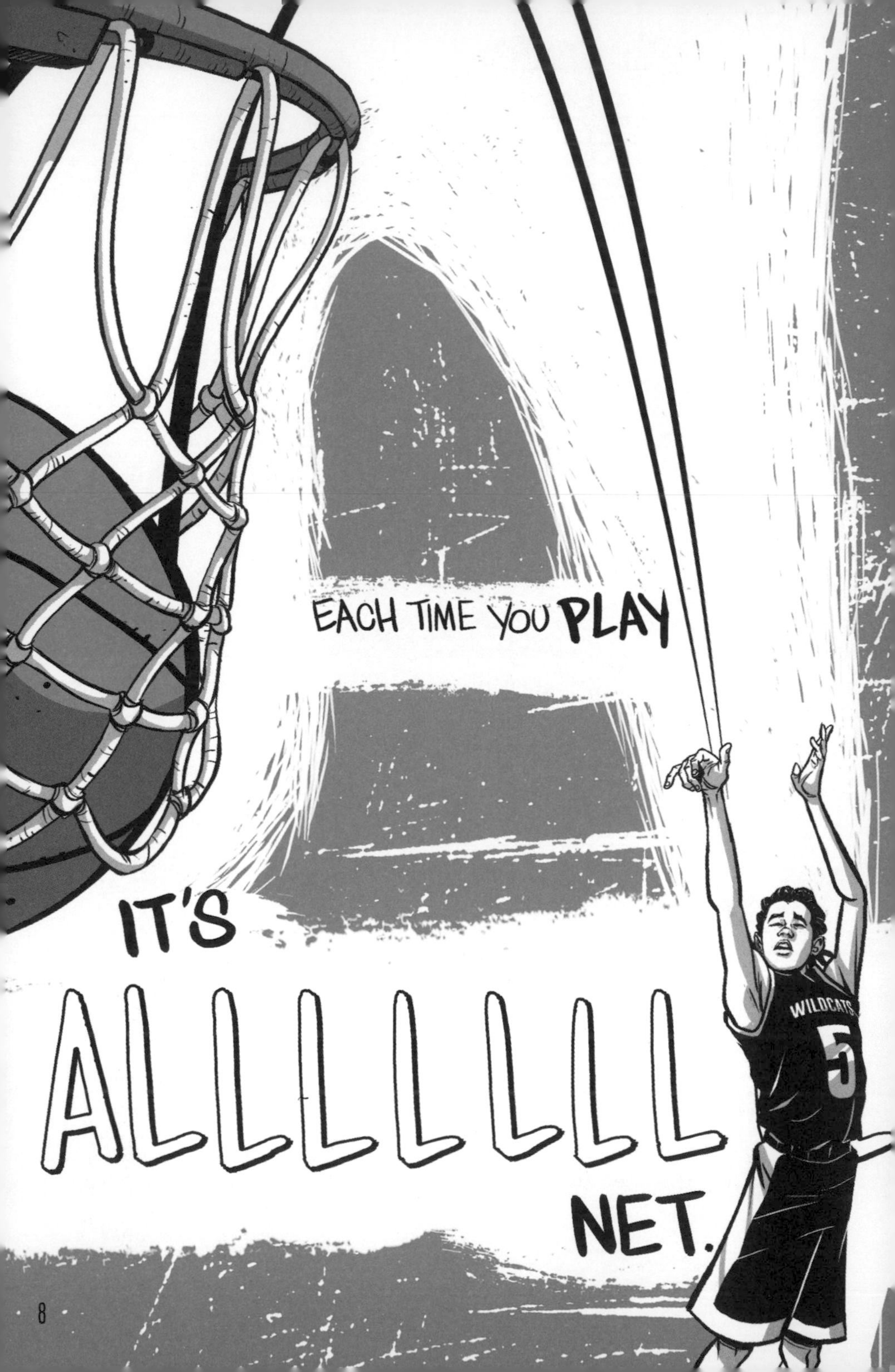
EACH TIME YOU PLAY
IT'S
ALLLLLLL
NET.
WILDCATS
5

IF ANYONE ELSE CALLED ME **FRESH** AND **SWEET**,

I'D BURN MAD AS A **FLAME**. BUT I KNOW SHE'S ONLY TALKING ABOUT **MY GAME**.

SEE, WHEN I PLAY BALL, I'M ON **FIRE**.

WHEN I SHOOT, I **INSPIRE**.

THE HOOP'S FOR SALE, AND I'M THE **BUYER**.

9

HOW I GOT MY NICKNAME

I'M NOT THAT BIG ON JAZZ MUSIC, BUT **DAD IS.**

ONE DAY WE WERE LISTENING TO A CD OF A **MUSICIAN** NAMED **HORACE SILVER,** AND DAD SAYS,

JOSH, THIS CAT IS THE REAL DEAL. LISTEN TO THAT PIANO, FAST AND **FREE,** JUST LIKE YOU AND **JB** ON THE **COURT.**

IT'S OKAY, I GUESS, DAD.

OKAY? DID YOU SAY **OKAY?**

BOY, YOU BETTER RECOGNIZE GREATNESS WHEN YOU HEAR IT. **HORACE SILVER** IS ONE OF THE **HIPPEST.** IF YOU SHOOT HALF AS GOOD AS HE **JAMS** —

DAD, NO ONE SAYS "HIPPEST" ANYMORE.

WELL, THEY OUGHT TO, 'CAUSE THIS **CAT** IS SO **HIP,** WHEN HE SITS DOWN HE'S STILL STANDING, HE SAYS.

REAL **FUNNY,** DAD.

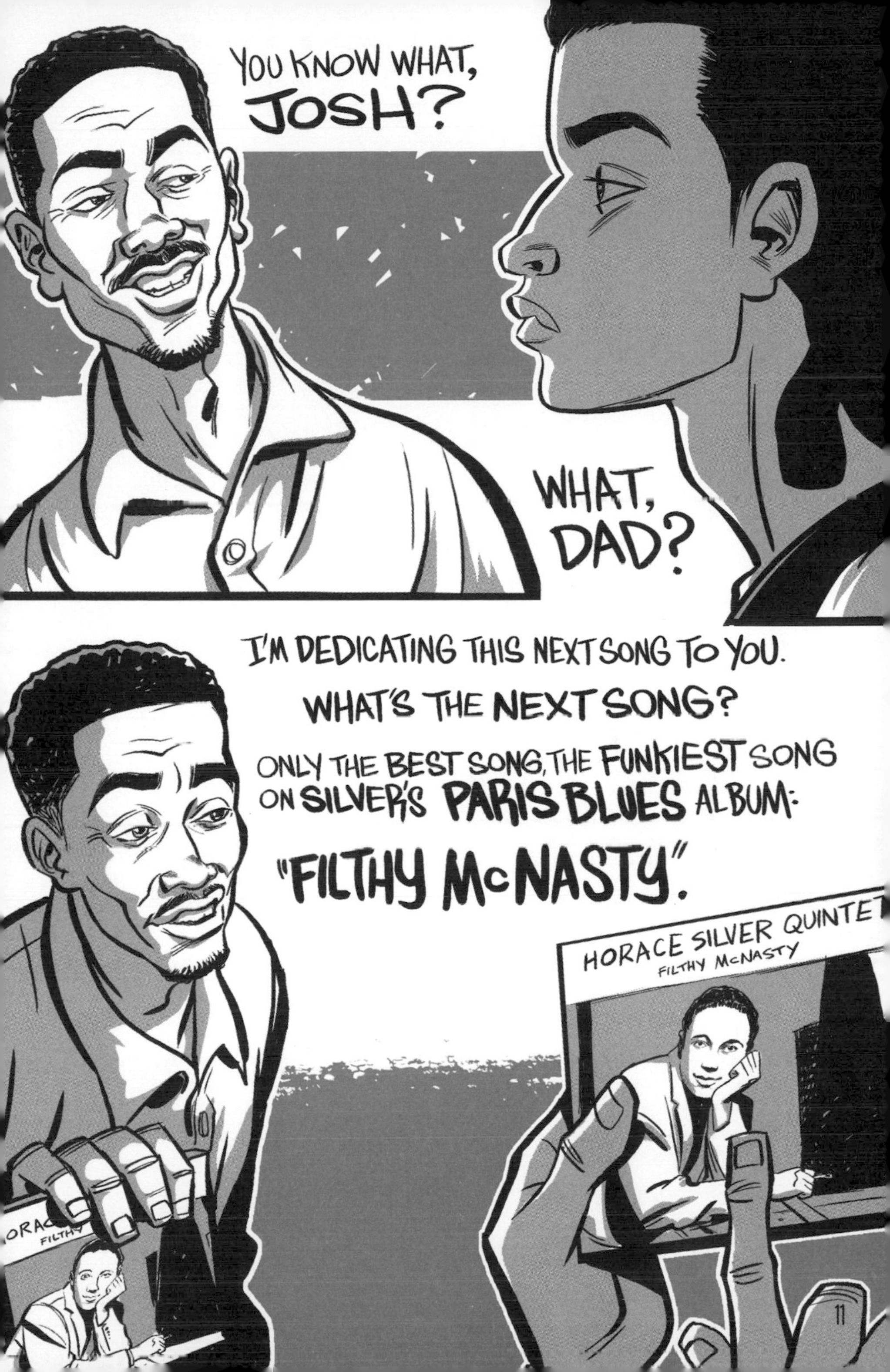
YOU KNOW WHAT, JOSH?
WHAT, DAD?
I'M DEDICATING THIS NEXT SONG TO YOU.
WHAT'S THE NEXT SONG?
ONLY THE BEST SONG, THE FUNKIEST SONG ON SILVER'S PARIS BLUES ALBUM:
"FILTHY McNASTY".
HORACE SILVER QUINTET
FILTHY McNASTY

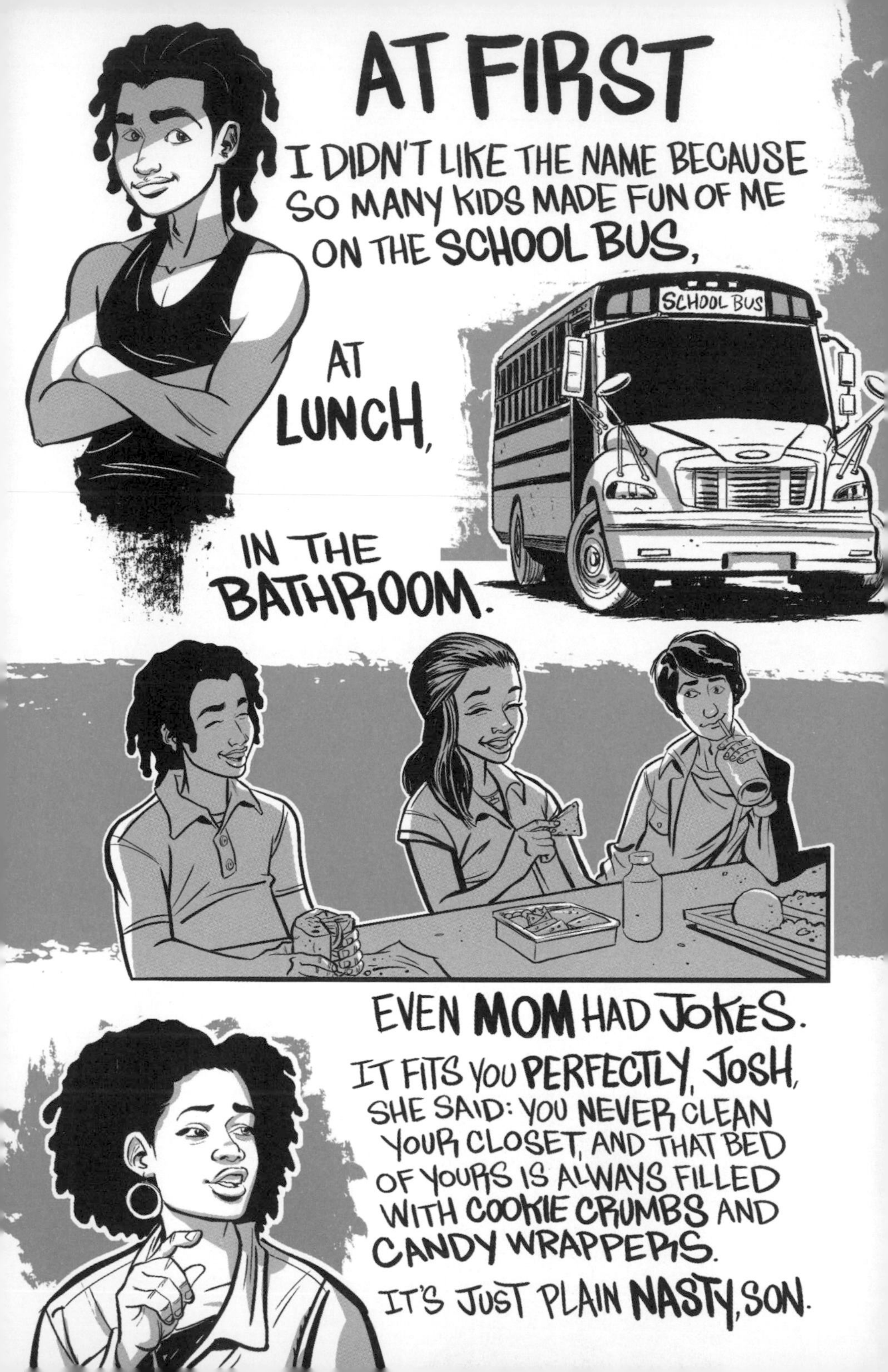
AT FIRST
I DIDN'T LIKE THE NAME BECAUSE SO MANY KIDS MADE FUN OF ME ON THE SCHOOL BUS,
SCHOOL BUS
AT LUNCH,
IN THE BATHROOM.
EVEN MOM HAD JOKES.
IT FITS YOU PERFECTLY, JOSH, SHE SAID: YOU NEVER CLEAN YOUR CLOSET, AND THAT BED OF YOURS IS ALWAYS FILLED WITH COOKIE CRUMBS AND CANDY WRAPPERS.
IT'S JUST PLAIN NASTY, SON.

BUT, AS I GOT **OLDER** AND STARTED GETTING GAME, THE NAME TOOK ON A NEW MEANING.

AND EVEN THOUGH I WASN'T INTO ALL THAT **JAZZ**, EVERY TIME I'D SCORE, REBOUND, OR **STEAL** A **BALL**, DAD WOULD JUMP UP **SMILING** AND **SCREAMIN'**,

THAT'S MY BOY OUT THERE, KEEP IT FUNKY, **FILTHY**!

AND THAT MADE ME FEEL REAL **GOOD** ABOUT MY **NICKNAME**.

13

FILTHY McNASTY

IS A **MYTHICAL MANCHILD** OF RATHER **DUBIOUS** DISTINCTION.

ALWAYS **AGITATING, COMBINATING,** AND **ELEVATING** HIS GAME.

HE DRIBBLES, FAKES, THEN TAKES THE **ROCK** TO THE GLASS, **FAST,** AND ON **BLAST.**

BUT WATCH OUT WHEN HE **SHOOTS** OR YOU'LL GET

SCHOOLED FOOLED UNCOOLED.

'CAUSE WHEN **FILTHY** GETS **HOT** HE HAS A

SLAMMERIFIC SHOT.

IT'S **DUNKALICIOUS CLASSY SUPERSONIC SASSY** AND **DOWNRIGHT** IN YOUR FACE **McNASTY.**

14

JORDAN BELL

MY TWIN BROTHER IS A **BALLER**.

THE ONLY THING HE LOVES MORE THAN BASKETBALL IS **BETTING**.

IF IT'S NINETY DEGREES OUTSIDE AND THE SKY IS **CLOUDLESS**, HE WILL BET YOU THAT IT'S GOING TO **RAIN**.

IT'S ANNOYING AND SOMETIMES **FUNNY**.

JORDAN INSISTS THAT EVERYONE CALL HIM **JB**.

HIS FAVORITE **PLAYER** IS **MICHAEL JORDAN**, BUT HE DOESN'T WANT PEOPLE TO THINK HE'S **SWEATING** HIM.

EVEN THOUGH **HE IS**.

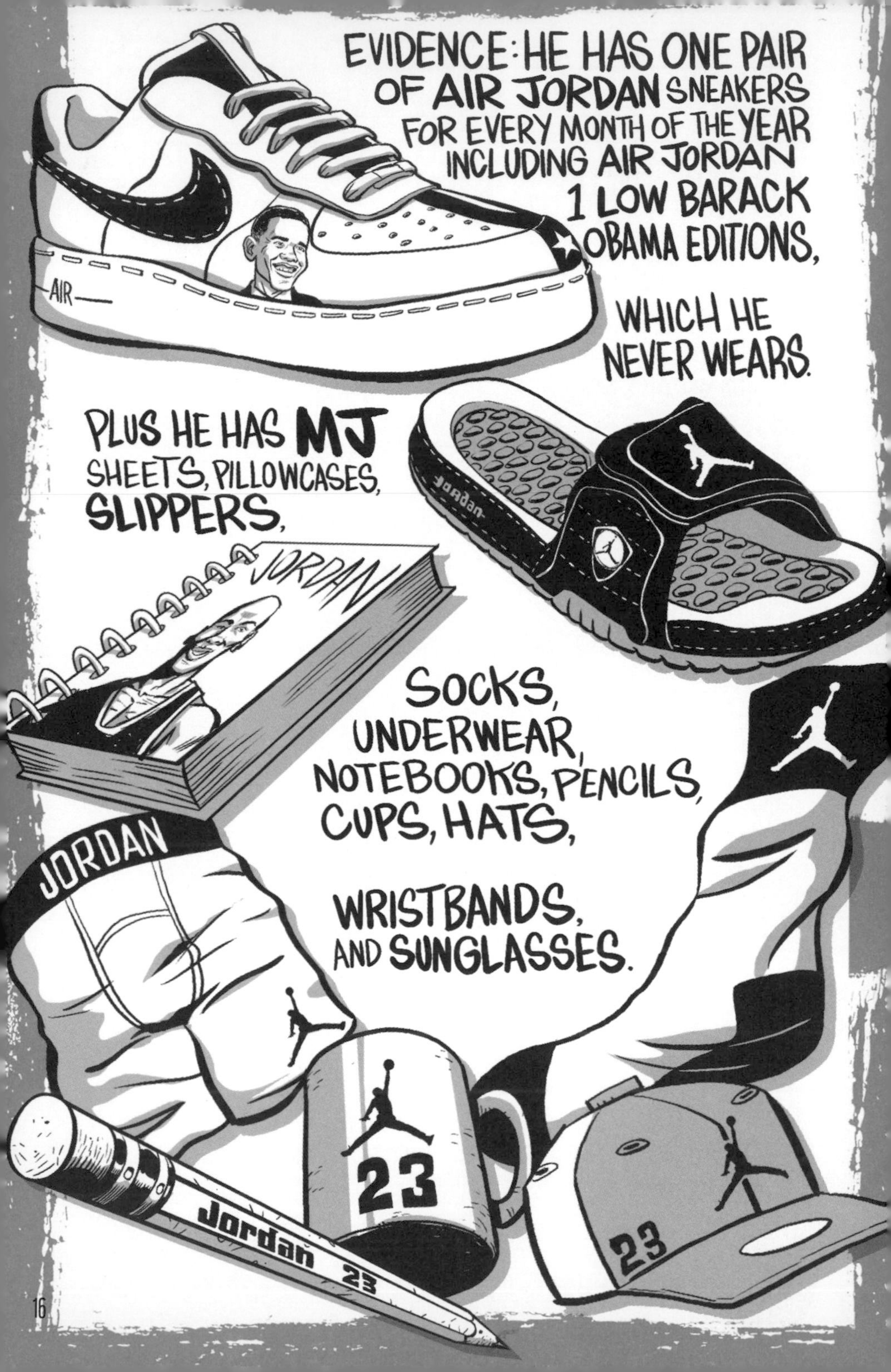
EVIDENCE: HE HAS ONE PAIR OF AIR JORDAN SNEAKERS FOR EVERY MONTH OF THE YEAR INCLUDING AIR JORDAN 1 LOW BARACK OBAMA EDITIONS,
WHICH HE NEVER WEARS.
AIR
PLUS HE HAS MJ SHEETS, PILLOWCASES, SLIPPERS,
JORDAN
JORDAN
SOCKS, UNDERWEAR, NOTEBOOKS, PENCILS, CUPS, HATS,
WRISTBANDS, AND SUNGLASSES.
JORDAN
23
Jordan 23
23

WITH THE FIFTY DOLLARS HE WON FROM A **BET** HE AND DAD MADE OVER WHETHER THE **KRISPY KREME** HOT SIGN WAS ON (IT WASN'T)

HE PURCHASED A **MICHAEL JORDAN** TOOTHBRUSH ("ONLY USED ONCE!") ON **eBAY.**

HE'S RIGHT, HE'S **NOT** SWEATING HIM.

HE'S **STALKING** HIM.

17

ON THE WAY TO THE GAME

I'M **BANISHED** TO THE BACK SEAT WITH **JB**, WHO ONLY STOPS PLAYING WITH MY **LOCKS**

WHEN I **SLAP** HIM ACROSS HIS **BALD HEAD** WITH MY **JOCKSTRAP**.

FIVE REASONS I HAVE LOCKS

5 SOME OF MY FAVORITE **RAPPERS** HAVE THEM:

LIL WAYNE

2 CHAINZ

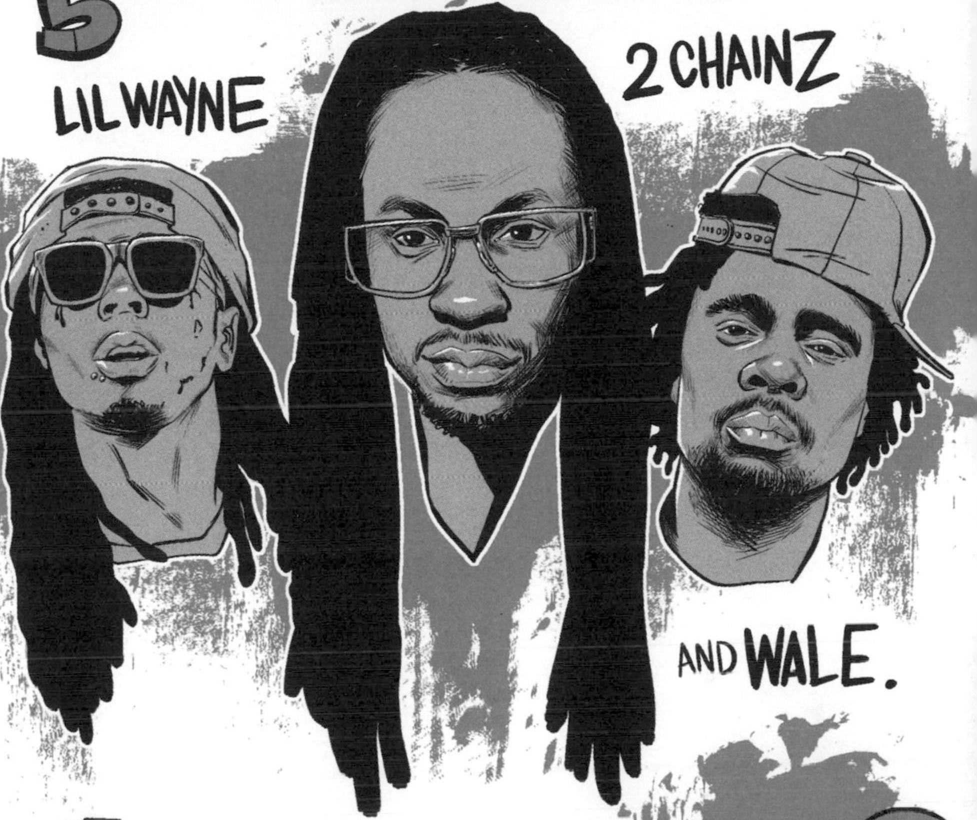

AND **WALE**.

4 THEY MAKE ME FEEL LIKE A **KING**.

3 NO ONE ELSE ON THE TEAM HAS THEM, AND

2 IT HELPS PEOPLE KNOW THAT I AM **ME**

AND NOT **JB**.

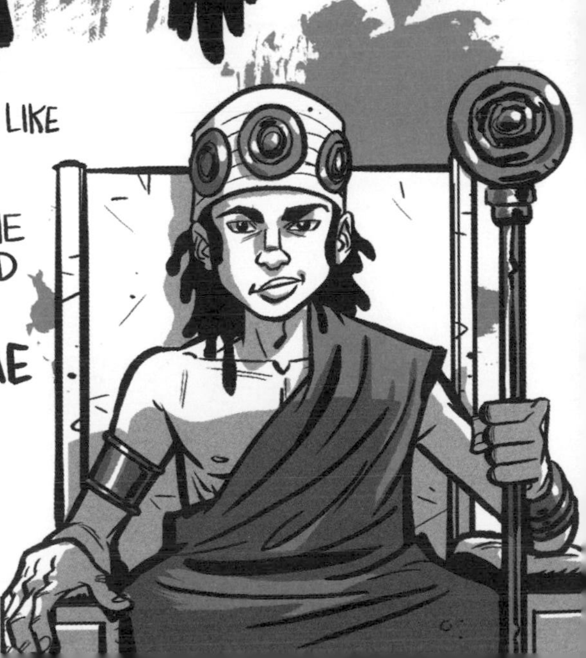

BUT **MOSTLY** BECAUSE

1 EVER SINCE I WATCHED THE CLIP OF DAD **POSTERIZING** THAT SEVEN-FOOT CROATIAN CENTER ON **ESPN'S BEST DUNKS EVER;**

SOARING THROUGH THE **AIR—** HIS **LONG** TWISTED HAIR LIKE **WINGS** CARRYING HIM HIGH ABOVE THE **RIM—**

I KNEW ONE DAY I'D NEED MY **OWN WINGS** TO **FLY.**

MOM TELLS DAD

THAT HE HAS TO SIT IN THE TOP ROW OF THE **BLEACHERS** DURING THE **GAME**.

YOU'RE TOO CONFRONTATIONAL, SHE SAYS.

FILTHY, DON'T FORGET TO FOLLOW THROUGH ON YOUR **JUMP SHOT**, DAD TELLS ME.

JB TELLS MOM, WE'RE ALMOST IN **HIGH SCHOOL**, SO NO **HUGS** BEFORE THE **GAME**, PLEASE.

DAD SAYS, YOU BOYS OUGHT TO **TREASURE** YOUR **MOTHER'S LOVE**.

MY **MOM** WAS LIKE **GOLD** TO ME.

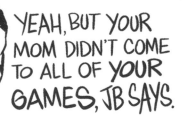

YEAH, BUT YOUR MOM DIDN'T COME TO ALL OF **YOUR** GAMES, JB SAYS.

AND SHE WASN'T THE **ASSISTANT** SCHOOL **PRINCIPAL** EITHER, I ADD.

CONVERSATION

DAD, DO YOU **MISS** PLAYING BASKETBALL? I ASK.

LIKE JAZZ MISSES DIZZY, HE SAYS.

HUH?

LIKE HIP-HOP MISSES TUPAC, FILTHY, HE SAYS.

OH! BUT YOU'RE STILL **YOUNG**,
YOU COULD PROBABLY STILL **PLAY**, RIGHT?

MY PLAYING DAYS ARE OVER, SON.
MY JOB NOW IS TO TAKE CARE OF THIS FAMILY.

DON'T YOU GET BORED SITTING AROUND THE HOUSE ALL DAY?
YOU COULD GET A JOB OR **SOMETHING**.

FILTHY, WHAT'S ALL THIS TALK ABOUT A JOB?

YOU DON'T THINK YOUR OL' MAN KNOWS
HOW TO HANDLE HIS BUSINESS?

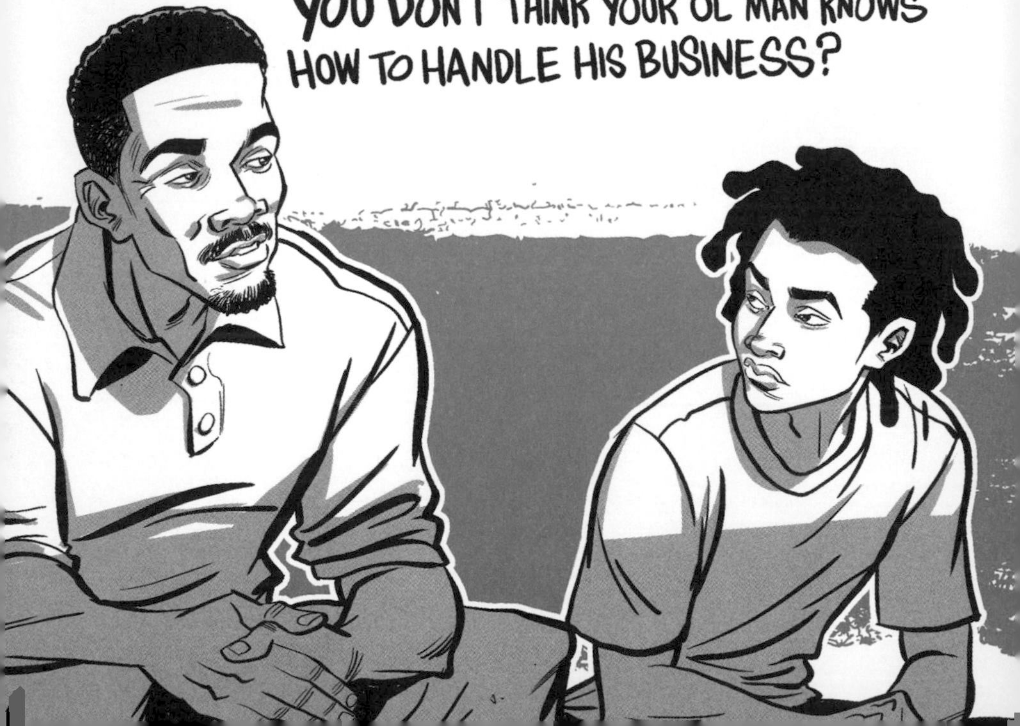

BOY, I SAVED MY **BASKETBALL MONEY** – THIS FAMILY IS FINE. YEAH, I MISS **BASKETBALL** A LOT, AND I DO HAVE SOME FEELERS OUT THERE ABOUT COACHING.

BUT HONESTLY, RIGHT NOW I'M FINE COACHING THIS HOUSE AND KEEPING UP WITH YOU **AND YOUR BROTHER.**

NOW GO GET **JB** SO WE WON'T BE LATE TO THE GAME AND COACH BENCHES YOU.

WHY DON'T YOU EVER WEAR YOUR CHAMPIONSHIP RING?

IS THIS JEOPARDY OR SOMETHING? WHAT'S WITH THE QUESTIONS? YEAH, I WEAR IT, WHEN I WANT TO FLOSS. DAD SMILES.

CAN I WEAR IT TO SCHOOL ONCE?

CAN YOU BOUNCE A BALL ON THE ROOF, OFF A TREE, IN THE HOOP?

UH… NO.
THEN, I GUESS YOU'RE NOT DA MAN. ONLY DA MAN WEARS **DA RING.**

AW, COME ON, DAD.

TELL YOU WHAT: YOU BRING HOME THE TROPHY THIS YEAR, AND WE'LL SEE.

THANKS, DAD. YOU KNOW, IF YOU GET BORED YOU COULD
ALWAYS WRITE A **BOOK**, LIKE **VONDIE'S** MOM DID.
SHE WROTE ONE ABOUT **SPACESHIPS**.

**A BOOK? WHAT WOULD YOU HAVE
ME WRITE ABOUT?**

MAYBE A BOOK OF THOSE RULES YOU GIVE
ME AND **JB** BEFORE EACH OF OUR **GAMES**.

I'M DA MAN BY CHUCK BELL,
DAD LAUGHS.

THAT'S **LAME**, DAD, I SAY.

WHO YOU CALLING
LAME? DAD SAYS,
HEADLOCKING ME.

DAD, TELL ME AGAIN
WHY THEY CALLED YOU
DA MAN?

FILTHY, BACK IN THE
DAY, I WAS THE **BOSS**,
NEVER LOST, I HAD THE
SICKEST DOUBLE CROSS,
AND I KISSED SO MANY
PRETTY LADIES, THEY
CALLED ME
LIP-GLOSS.

OH, REALLY? MOM SAYS,
SNEAKING UP ON US
LIKE SHE ALWAYS
SEEMS TO DO.

YEAH, YOU **DA MAN**, DAD,
I LAUGH, THEN THROW MY
GYM BAG IN THE **TRUNK**.

BASKETBALL RULE #1

IN THIS GAME OF LIFE YOUR FAMILY IS THE COURT AND THE BALL IS YOUR **HEART**.

NO MATTER HOW GOOD YOU ARE, NO MATTER HOW **DOWN** YOU GET, ALWAYS LEAVE YOUR HEART ON THE **COURT**.

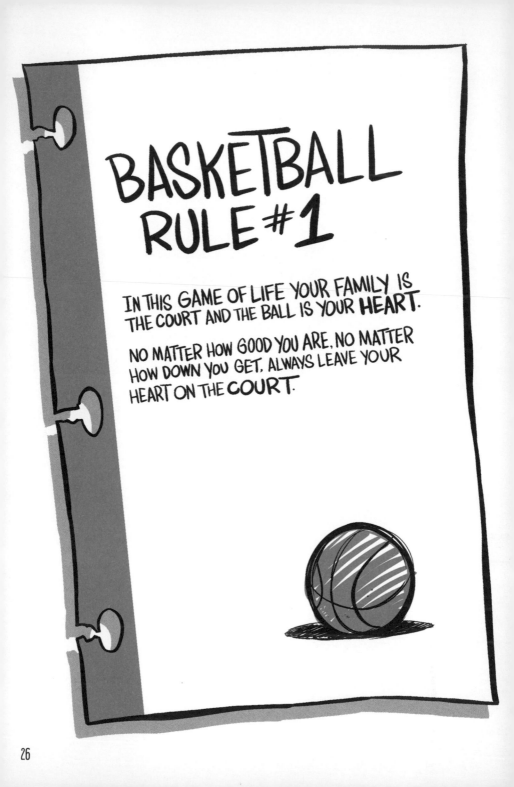

FIRST QUARTER

JB AND I

ARE ALMOST **THIRTEEN**. **TWINS**. TWO BASKETBALL GOALS AT OPPOSITE ENDS OF THE **COURT**.

IDENTICAL. IT'S EASY TO TELL US APART THOUGH.

I'M AN INCH TALLER, WITH **DREADS** TO MY NECK.

HE GETS HIS HEAD **SHAVED** ONCE A **MONTH**.

I WANT TO GO TO **DUKE**.

HE **FLAUNTS CAROLINA BLUE**.

IF WE DIDN'T **LOVE** EACH OTHER, WE'D **HATE** EACH OTHER.

29

HE'S A SHOOTING GUARD. I PLAY FORWARD. JB'S THE SECOND MOST PHENOMENAL BALLER ON OUR **TEAM**.

HE HAS THE BETTER **JUMPER**, BUT I'M THE BETTER **SLASHER**. AND MUCH **FASTER**. WE BOTH PASS WELL. ESPECIALLY TO EACH OTHER.

TO GET READY FOR THE SEASON, I WENT TO THREE **SUMMER CAMPS**.

JB ONLY WENT TO **ONE**. SAID HE DIDN'T WANT TO MISS **BIBLE SCHOOL**.

WHAT DOES HE THINK, I'M **STUPID?**

EVER SINCE **KIM BAZEMORE** KISSED HIM IN **SUNDAY SCHOOL**, HE'S BEEN ACTING ALL **RELIGIOUS**, THINKING LESS AND **LESS** ABOUT **BASKETBALL**, AND **MORE** AND **MORE** ABOUT **GIRLS**.

AT THE END OF WARM-UPS, MY BROTHER TRIES TO DUNK

NOT EVEN CLOSE, JB.
WHAT'S THE MATTER?
THE HOOP TOO HIGH FOR YOU?

I SNICKER BUT IT'S NOT FUNNY TO HIM, ESPECIALLY WHEN I TAKE OFF FROM CENTER COURT, MY HAIR LIKE WINGS, EACH LOCK LIFTING ME HIGHER AND HIGHER, LIKE A 747.

CLANK!

ZOOM!

ZOOM!

I THROW DOWN SO **HARD**, THE FIBERGLASS **TREMBLES.**

BOO YAH!

DAD SCREAMS FROM THE **TOP ROW.**

I'M THE **ONLY** KID ON THE TEAM WHO CAN DO THAT.

THE **HARD** IS A LOUD, CROWDED **CIRCUS.**
MY STOMACH IS A **ROLLER COASTER.**

MY HEAD, A **CAROUSEL.**
THE **AIR**, HEAVY WITH THE SMELL OF **SWEAT**, POPCORN, AND THE **SWEET** PERFUME OF **MOTHERS** WATCHING **SONS.**

OUR MOM, A.K.A. DR. BELL, A.K.A. THE ASSISTANT PRINCIPAL, IS TALKING TO SOME OF THE **TEACHERS** ON THE OTHER SIDE OF THE **GYM.**

I'M FEELING BETTER ALREADY.

COACH CALLS US IN, DOES HIS **PHIL JACKSON** IMPERSONATION.

LOVE **IGNITES** THE **SPIRIT,** BRINGS TEAMS TOGETHER, HE SAYS.

JB AND I GLANCE AT EACH OTHER, READY TO BUST OUT **LAUGHING,** BUT **VONDIE,** OUR BEST FRIEND, BEATS US TO IT.

THE WHISTLE GOES OFF.

PLAYERS GATHER AT CENTER CIRCLE, **DAP** EACH OTHER, POUND EACH OTHER.

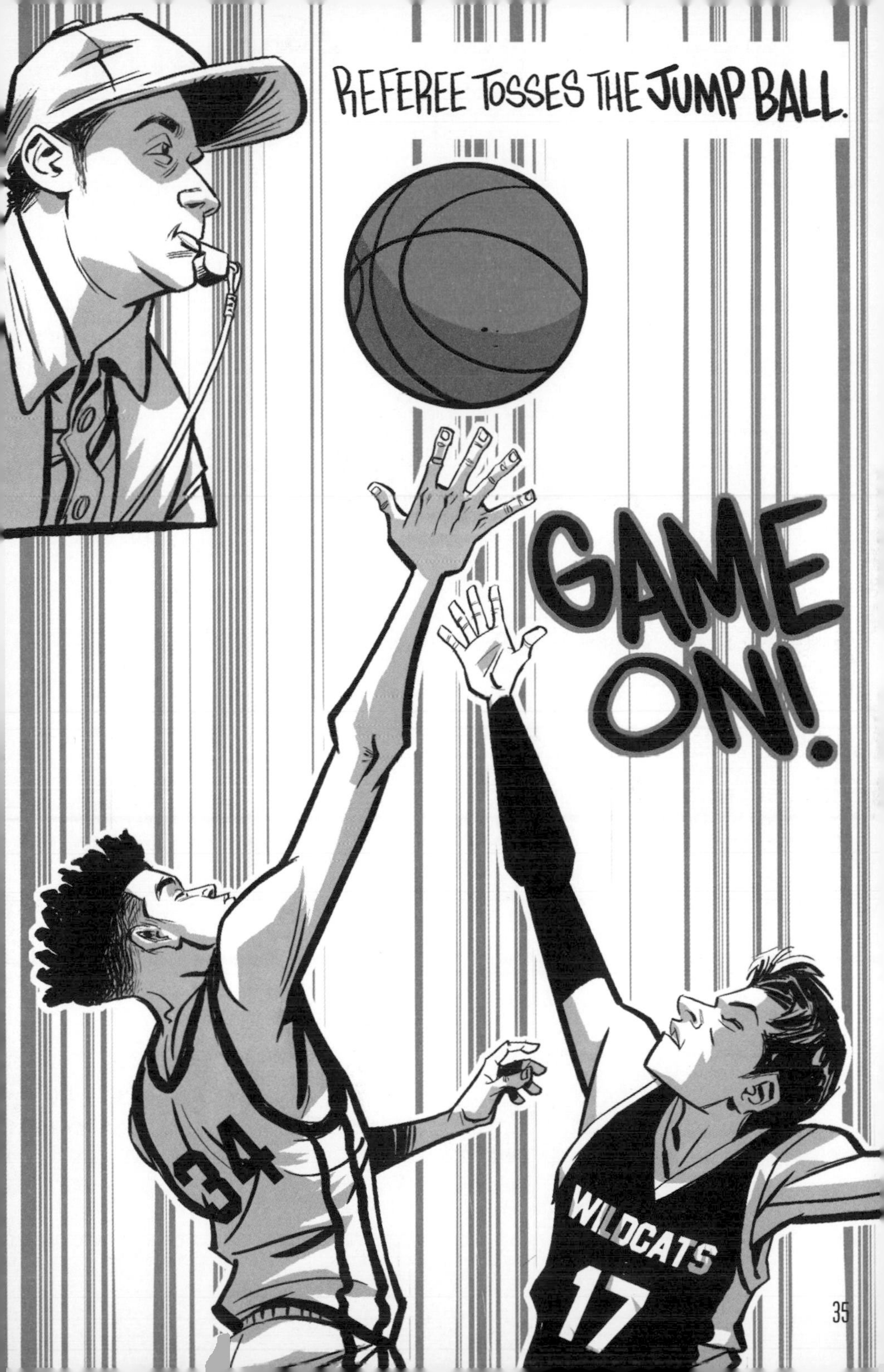
REFEREE TOSSES THE JUMP BALL.
GAME ON!
34
WILDCATS
17

THE SPORTSCASTER

JB LIKES TO TAUNT AND TRASH TALK DURING GAMES LIKE DAD USED TO DO WHEN HE **PLAYED.**

WHEN I WALK ONTO THE COURT I PREFER SILENCE SO I CAN

WATCH

REACT

SURPRISE.

I TALK TOO, BUT MOSTLY TO MYSELF, LIKE SOMETIMES WHEN I DO MY OWN PLAY-BY-PLAY IN MY HEAD.

JOSH'S PLAY-BY-PLAY

IT'S GAME **THREE** FOR THE
TWO-AND-OH WILDCATS.
NUMBER **SEVENTEEN**,
VONDIE LITTLE, GRABS IT.

NOTHING LITTLE ABOUT THAT **KID**.
THE WILDCATS HAVE IT, FIRST
PLAY OF THE **GAME**.

THE HOPES ARE **HIGH** TONIGHT
AT **REGGIE LEWIS JUNIOR HIGH**.

WE **DESTROYED** HOOVER MIDDLE
LAST WEEK, THIRTY-TWO TO **FOUR**,
AND WE WON'T **STOP**, CAN'T **STOP**,
TILL WE CLAIM THE
CHAMPIONSHIP TROPHY.

VONDIE OVERHEAD PASSES ME. I
FLING A QUICK CHEST PASS TO MY **TWIN**
BROTHER, **JB**, NUMBER **TWENTY-THREE**,
A.K.A. THE **JUMPER.**

I'VE SEEN HIM LAUNCH IT FROM
THIRTY FEET BEFORE,

ALL NET.

37

THAT BOY IS **SPECIAL**,

AND IT DOESN'T HURT THAT CHUCK "DA MAN" BELL IS HIS **FATHER**.

AND **MINE**, TOO.

JB BOUNCES THE BALL BACK TO ME.

JB'S A SHOOTER, BUT I'M **SNEAKY** AND **SILKY** AS A SNAKE — AND YOU THOUGHT MY **HAIR** WAS **LONG**.

I'M **SIX FEET**, ALL **LEGS**.

OH, WOW-DID YOU SEE THAT NASTY CROSSOVER?

NOW YOU SEE WHY THEY CALL ME **FILTHY**.

FOLKS, I HOPE YOU GOT YOUR TICKETS, BECAUSE I'M ABOUT TO PUT ON A **SHOW**.

CROSS·O·VER

[KRAWS-OH-VER] NOUN

A SIMPLE BASKETBALL MOVE IN WHICH A **PLAYER DRIBBLES** THE BALL **QUICKLY** FROM ONE **HAND** TO THE **OTHER**.

AS IN: WHEN DONE RIGHT, A **CROSSOVER** CAN **BREAK** AN **OPPONENT'S ANKLES**.

AS IN: **DERON WILLIAMS'S** CROSSOVER IS NICE.

BUT **ALLEN IVERSON'S** CROSSOVER WAS SO **DEADLY**, HE COULD'VE SET UP HIS **OWN** PODIATRY **PRACTICE**.

AS IN: DAD TAUGHT ME HOW TO GIVE A **SOFT** CROSS FIRST TO SEE IF YOUR **OPPONENT** FALLS FOR IT,

THEN HIT 'EM WITH THE HARD **CROSSOVER**.

THE SHOW

A QUICK SHOULDER SHAKE,
A SLICK EYE **FAKE**—
NUMBER 28 IS WAY PAST **LATE**.

HE'S READING ME LIKE A **BOOK**,
BUT I TURN THE PAGE AND WATCH HIM
LOOK, WHICH CAN ONLY MEAN I GOT
HIM **SHOOK**.

HIS FEET ARE THE **BANK** AND I'M THE CROOK.

BREAKING, BRAKING,
TAKING HIM TO THE LEFT—
NOW HE'S **TOOK**.

NUMBER 14 JOINS IN...NOW HE'S
ON THE **HOOK**.

I GOT **TWO** IN MY KITCHEN AND I'M
FIXING TO **COOK**.

PREPPIN' MY **MEAL**,
READY FOR GLASS...

NOBODY'S EXPECTING
FILTHY TO PASS. I SEE
VONDIE UNDER THE
HOOP SO I
SERVE
HIM UP
MY

Alley-

OOP.

THE BET, PART ONE

WE'RE DOWN BY SEVEN AT HALFTIME.
TROUBLE OWNS OUR FACES BUT COACH ISN'T WORRIED.
SAYS WE HAVEN'T FOUND OUR RHYTHM YET.

THEN, ALL OF A
SUDDEN, OUT OF
NOWHERE VONDIE
STARTS DANCING
THE SNAKE, ONLY
HE LOOKS LIKE A
SEAL.

THEN COACH BLASTS HIS FAVORITE
DANCE MUSIC, AND BEFORE YOU
KNOW IT WE'RE ALL DOING THE
CHA-CHA SLIDE:

TO THE LEFT, TAKE IT
BACK NOW Y'ALL.
ONE HOP THIS TIME,
RIGHT FOOT LET'S STOMP.

JB HIGH-FIVES ME,
WITH A FAMILIAR LOOK.

YOU WANT TO BET, DON'T YOU? I ASK.

YEP, HE SAYS, THEN TOUCHES MY HAIR.

ODE TO MY HAIR

IF MY HAIR WERE A TREE I'D **CLIMB IT.**

I'D KNEEL DOWN BENEATH AND **ENSHRINE IT.**

I'D TREAT IT LIKE **GOLD** AND THEN **MINE IT.**

EACH DAY BEFORE SCHOOL
I **UNWIND IT.**

AND RIGHT BEFORE **GAMES**
I **ENTWINE IT.**

THESE LOCKS ON MY
HEAD, I **DESIGNED IT.**

AND ONE LAST THING IF
YOU DON'T **MIND IT:**

THAT BET YOU JUST
MADE?

I **DECLINE IT.**

THE BET, PART TWO

IF. I. LOSE. THE. BET. YOU. WANT. TO. WHAT?

IF THE SCORE GETS TIED, HE SAYS, AND IF IT COMES DOWN TO THE **LAST SHOT**, HE SAYS, AND IF I GET THE BALL, HE SAYS, AND IF I DON'T **MISS**, HE SAYS, I GET TO CUT OFF **YOUR HAIR**.

SURE, I SAY, AS SERIOUS AS A HEART ATTACK. YOU CAN CUT MY **LOCKS** OFF, BUT IF I WIN THE BET YOU HAVE TO WALK AROUND WITH NO PANTS ON AND NO **UNDERWEAR** TOMORROW IN SCHOOL DURING **LUNCH**.

VONDIE AND THE REST OF THE FELLAS LAUGH LIKE **HYENAS**.

NOT TO BE OUTDONE, **JB** REVISES THE **BET**:

OKAY, HE SAYS.

HOW ABOUT IF YOU LOSE I CUT **ONE** LOCK AND IF YOU WIN I WILL **MOON** THAT **NERDY** GROUP OF SIXTH-GRADERS THAT SIT NEAR OUR TABLE AT **LUNCH**?

EVEN THOUGH I USED TO BE ONE OF THOSE **NERDY** SIXTH-GRADERS, EVEN THOUGH I LOVE MY HAIR THE WAY DAD LOVES **KRISPY KREME**, EVEN THOUGH I DON'T WANT US TO **LOSE** THE GAME, ODDS ARE THIS IS ONE OF **JB'S** LEGENDARY BETS **I'LL WIN**, BECAUSE THAT'S A LOT OF *IFS*.

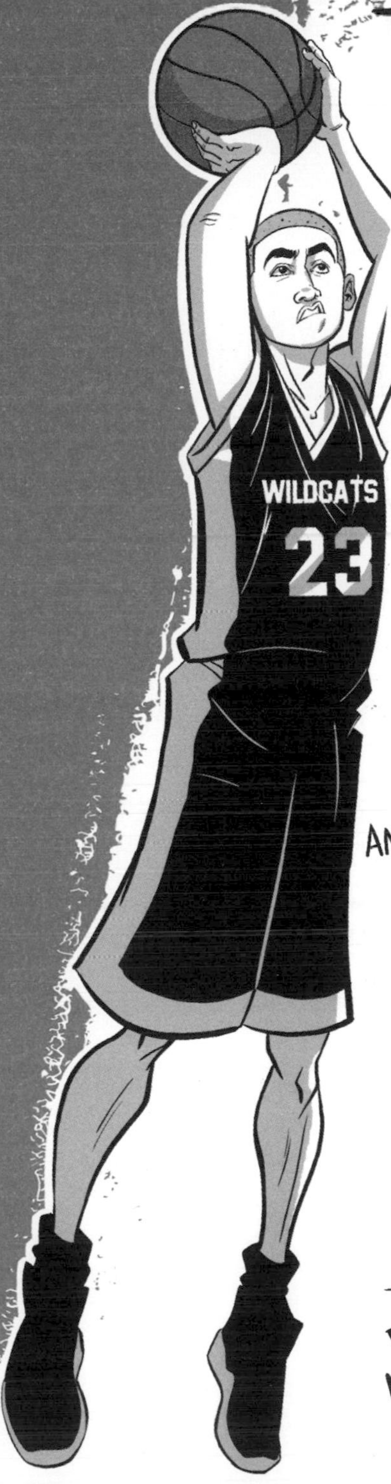
WILDCATS
23

THE GAME IS TIED

WHEN JB'S SOFT JUMPER SAILS

Tick

THROUGH THE **AIR**.

Tock

THE CROWD STILLS,

Tick

MOUTHS **DROP**,

Tock

AND WHEN HIS LAST-SECOND SHOT

Tick

HITS **NET**,

Tock

THE **CLOCK** STOPS.

THE GYM EXPLODES. ITS HARD
BLEACHERS EMPTY AND MY
HEAD ACHES.

IN THE LOCKER ROOM

AFTER THE GAME, **JB** CACKLES LIKE A CROW. HE WALKS UP TO ME GRINNING, HOLDS HIS HAND OUT SO I CAN SEE THE RED SCISSORS FROM COACH'S DESK SMILING AT ME, THEIR STEEL BLADES **SHARP** AND **READY**.

I LOVE THIS GAME LIKE THE WINTER LOVES SNOW EVEN THOUGH I SPENT THE FINAL QUARTER IN FOUL TROUBLE ON THE **BENCH**.

JB WAS ON **FIRE** AND WE **WON** AND I **LOST** THE **BET**.

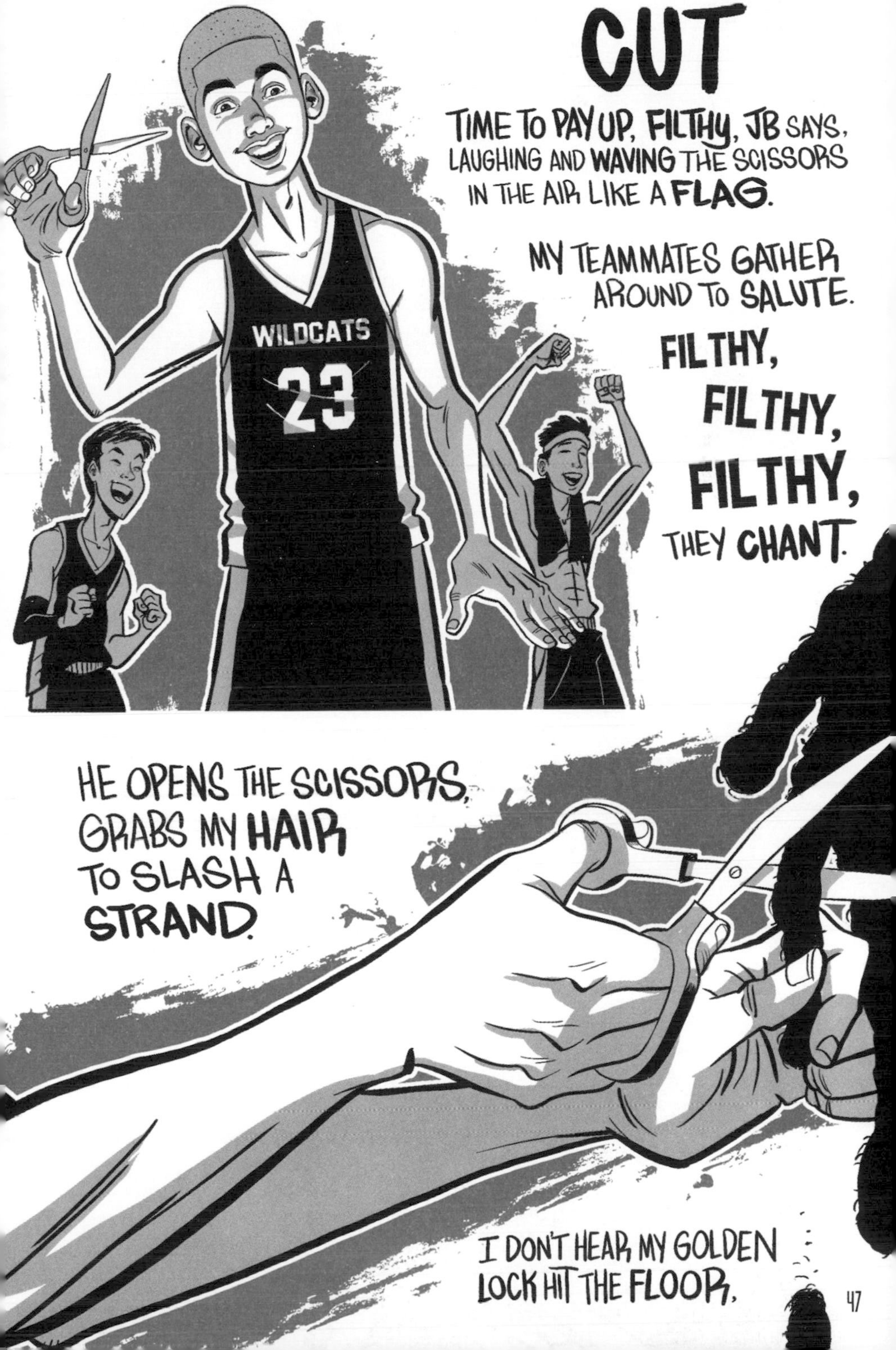
CUT
TIME TO PAY UP, FILTHY, JB SAYS,
LAUGHING AND WAVING THE SCISSORS
IN THE AIR LIKE A FLAG.
MY TEAMMATES GATHER
AROUND TO SALUTE.
FILTHY,
FILTHY,
FILTHY,
THEY CHANT.
WILDCATS
23
HE OPENS THE SCISSORS,
GRABS MY HAIR
TO SLASH A
STRAND.
I DON'T HEAR MY GOLDEN
LOCK HIT THE FLOOR.

BUT I DO HEAR THE SOUND OF CALAMITY WHEN VONDIE HOLLERS,

OH, SNAP!

CA·LAM·I·TY
[KUH-LAM-IH-TEE] NOUN

AN UNEXPECTED, UNDESIRABLE EVENT; OFTEN PHYSICALLY INJURIOUS.

AS IN: IF **JB** HADN'T BEEN ACTING SO SILLY AND PLAYING AROUND, HE WOULD HAVE CUT ONE LOCK INSTEAD OF **FIVE** FROM MY HEAD AND AVOIDED THIS **CALAMITY.**

AS IN: THE **HUGE** BALD PATCH ON THE SIDE OF MY **HEAD** IS A DREADFUL **CALAMITY.**

AS IN: AFTER THE GAME MOM ALMOST HAS A FIT WHEN SHE SEES MY **HAIR.**

WHAT A **CALAMITY,** SHE SAYS, SHAKING HER HEAD AND TELLING DAD TO TAKE ME TO THE BARBER SHOP ON SATURDAY TO HAVE THE REST CUT OFF.

MOM DOESN'T LIKE US EATING OUT

BUT ONCE A MONTH SHE LETS ONE OF US CHOOSE A RESTAURANT AND EVEN THOUGH SHE WON'T LET HIM TOUCH HALF THE THINGS ON THE BUFFET, IT'S DAD'S TURN AND HE CHOOSES **CHINESE**.

I KNOW WHAT HE REALLY WANTS IS **POLLARD'S CHICKEN** AND **BBQ**, BUT MOM HAS BANNED US FROM THAT PLACE.

IN THE **GOLDEN DRAGON**, MOM IS STILL FROWNING AT **JB** FOR MESSING UP MY **HAIR**.

BUT, MOM, IT WAS AN ACCIDENT, HE SAYS.

ACCIDENT OR NOT, YOU OWE YOUR BROTHER AN **APOLOGY**, SHE TELLS HIM.

I'M SORRY FOR CUTTING YOUR FILTHY HAIR, **FILTHY**, **JB** LAUGHS.

NOT SO **FUNNY** NOW, IS IT? I SAY, MY KNUCKLES DIGGING INTO HIS **SCALP** TILL DAD SAVES HIM FROM THE **NOOGIE** WITH ONE OF HIS **LAME JOKES**:

WHY CAN'T YOU PLAY SPORTS IN THE **JUNGLE**? HE ASKS.

MOM REPEATS THE QUESTION BECAUSE DAD WON'T CONTINUE UNTIL SOMEONE DOES.

BECAUSE OF THE CHEETAHS, HE SNAPS BACK, SO AMUSED, HE ALMOST FALLS OUT OF HIS CHAIR, WHICH CAUSES ALL OF US TO LAUGH, AND GET PAST MY HAIR ISSUE FOR NOW.

I FILL MY PLATE WITH **EGG ROLLS** AND **DUMPLINGS**.

JB ASKS DAD HOW WE DID.

Y'ALL DID OKAY, DAD SAYS, BUT, JB, WHY DID YOU LET THAT KID POST YOU UP?

AND, **FILTHY**, WHAT WAS UP WITH THAT LAZY **CROSSOVER**?

WHEN I WAS PLAYING, WE **NEVER**...

AND WHILE DAD IS TELLING US ANOTHER STORY FOR THE **HUNDREDTH TIME,**

MOM REMOVES THE **SALT** FROM THE TABLE AND **JB** GOES TO THE **BUFFET.**

HE BRINGS BACK THREE PACKAGES OF **DUCK SAUCE** AND A CUP OF WONTON SOUP AND HANDS THEM ALL TO ME.

DAD PAUSES, AND MOM LOOKS AT **JB.**

THAT WAS **RANDOM,** SHE SAYS.

WHAT, ISN'T THAT WHAT YOU WANTED, **FILTHY?** JB ASKS.

AND EVEN THOUGH I **NEVER** OPENED MY MOUTH, I SAY, THANKS, BECAUSE IT IS.

MISSING

I AM NOT A MATHEMATICIAN—A+B SELDOM EQUALS C.
PLUSES AND MINUSES, WE GET ALONG BUT WE ARE NOT CLOSE.

I AM NO **PYTHAGORAS.**

AND SO EACH TIME I COUNT THE LOCKS OF HAIR
BENEATH MY PILLOW I END UP WITH THIRTY-SEVEN
PLUS ONE TEAR, WHICH NEVER ADDS UP.

THE INSIDE OF MOM AND DAD'S BEDROOM CLOSET

IS OFF-LIMITS, SO EVERY TIME **JB** ASKS ME TO GO IN THERE TO LOOK
THROUGH DAD'S STUFF, I SAY **NO.** BUT TODAY WHEN I ASK MOM FOR
A BOX TO PUT MY **DREADLOCKS** IN, SHE TELLS ME TO TAKE
ONE OF HER **SUNDAY** HAT BOXES FROM THE TOP SHELF OF HER CLOSET.

NEXT TO HER PURPLE HAT BOX IS DAD'S SMALL SILVER SAFETY BOX
WITH THE KEY IN THE LOCK AND PRACTICALLY BEGGING ME TO OPEN IT,
SO I DO, WHEN, UNEXPECTEDLY:

WHAT ARE YOU DOING, **FILTHY?**

STANDING IN THE DOORWAY IS **JB** WITH A LOOK THAT SAYS **BUSTED!**

FILTHY, YOU STILL GIVING ME THE SILENT **TREATMENT?**

. . .

I REALLY AM SORRY ABOUT YOUR HAIR, MAN. I OWE YOU, **FILTHY,** SO I'M GONNA CUT THE GRASS FOR THE REST OF THE **YEAR** AND PICK UP THE LEAVES...AND I'LL WASH THE CARS AND I'LL EVEN **WASH** YOUR HAIR.

OH, YOU GOT JOKES, HUH? I SAY, THEN GRAB HIM AND GIVE HIM ANOTHER **NOOGIE.**

SO, WHAT ARE YOU DOING IN HERE, **FILTHY?**

NOTHING, MOM SAID I COULD USE HER HAT BOX. THAT DOESN'T LOOK LIKE A HAT BOX, FILTHY. LET ME SEE THAT, HE SAYS.

AND JUST LIKE THAT WE'RE RUMMAGING THROUGH A BOX FILLED WITH NEWSPAPER **CLIPPINGS ABOUT CHUCK "DA MAN" BELL** AND TORN TICKET STUBS AND OLD FLYERS AND...

WHOA !

THERE IT IS, FILTHY, JB SAYS.

AND EVEN THOUGH WE'VE SEEN DAD WEAR IT MANY TIMES, ACTUALLY HOLDING HIS GLOSSY CHAMPIONSHIP RING IN OUR HANDS IS MORE THAN MAGICAL.

LET'S TRY IT ON, I WHISPER.

BUT JB IS A STEP AHEAD, ALREADY SLIDING IT ON EACH OF HIS FINGERS UNTIL HE FINDS ONE IT FITS.

WHAT ELSE IS IN THERE, JB? I ASK, HOPING HE WILL REALIZE IT'S MY TURN TO WEAR DAD'S CHAMPIONSHIP RING.

THERE'S A BUNCH OF ARTICLES ABOUT DAD'S TRIPLE-DOUBLES, THREE-POINT RECORDS, AND THE TIME HE MADE FIFTY FREE THROWS IN A ROW AT THE OLYMPIC FINALS, HE SAYS, FINALLY HANDING ME THE RING, AND AN ITALIAN ARTICLE ABOUT DAD'S BELLISSIMO CROSSOVER AND HIS MILLION-DOLLAR MULTIYEAR CONTRACT WITH THE EUROPEAN LEAGUE.

PRIVATE

WE ALREADY KNOW ALL THIS STUFF, JB. ANYTHING NEW, OR SECRET-TYPE STUFF? I ASK. AND THEN JB PULLS OUT A MANILA ENVELOPE. I GRAB IT, GLANCE AT THE PRIVATE STAMPED ON THE FRONT. IN THE MOMENT THAT I DECIDE TO PUT IT BACK, JB SNATCHES IT.

LET'S DO THIS, HE SAYS. I RESIST, READY TO TAKE THE PURPLE HAT BOX AND JET, BUT I GUESS THE MYSTERY IS JUST TOO MUCH.

WE OPEN IT. THERE ARE TWO LETTERS. THE FIRST LETTER READS:
"CHUCK BELL, THE LOS ANGELES LAKERS WOULD LIKE TO INVITE YOU TO OUR FREE-AGENT TRYOUTS."

WE OPEN THE OTHER. IT STARTS: "YOUR DECISION NOT TO HAVE SURGERY MEANS THAT REALISTICALLY, WITH PATELLAR TENDONITIS, YOU MAY NOT BE ABLE TO PLAY AGAIN."

PA·TEL·LAR TEN·DO·NI·TIS
[PUH·TEL·AR TEN·DUH·NAHY·TIS] NOUN

THE CONDITION THAT ARISES WHEN THE MUSCLE THAT CONNECTS THE KNEECAP TO THE SHIN BONE BECOMES IRRITATED DUE TO OVERUSE, ESPECIALLY FROM JUMPING ACTIVITIES.

AS IN: ON THE TOP SHELF OF MOM AND DAD'S CLOSET IN A SILVER SAFETY BOX **JB** AND I DISCOVERED THAT MY DAD HAS **JUMPER'S KNEE**, A.K.A. PATELLAR TENDONITIS.

AS IN: AS A ROOKIE, MY DAD LED HIS TEAM TO THE **EUROLEAGUE** CHAMPIONSHIP, BUT THANKS TO **PATELLAR** TENDONITIS, HE WENT FROM A SUPERSTAR WITH A MILLION-DOLLAR **FADEAWAY** JUMPER TO A STAR WHOSE CAREER HAD **FADED** AWAY.

AS IN: I WONDER WHY MY DAD NEVER HAD **SURGERY** ON HIS **PATELLAR** TENDONITIS.

SUNDAYS AFTER CHURCH

WHEN THE PRAYERS END AND THE DOORS OPEN THE BELLS HIT CENTER STAGE AND THE CURTAIN OPENS UP ON THE AFTERNOON PICK-UP GAME IN THE GYM AT THE COUNTY RECREATION CENTER.

THE CAST IS FULL OF REGULARS AND ROOKIES WITH CARTOON NAMES LIKE FLAPJACK, SCOOBS, AND COOKIE. THE HIP-HOP SOUNDTRACK BLASTS. THE BASS BOOMS.

THE CROWD LOOMS. THERE'S MUSIC AND MOCKING, TEASING NONSTOP, BUT WHEN THE PLAY BEGINS ALL THE TALK CEASES.

DAD SHOVEL-PASSES THE BALL TO ME. I BEHIND-THE-BACK PASS TO JB, WHO SINKS A **TWENTY-FOOT THREE**.

SEE, THIS IS HOW WE ACT SUNDAYS AFTER CHURCH.

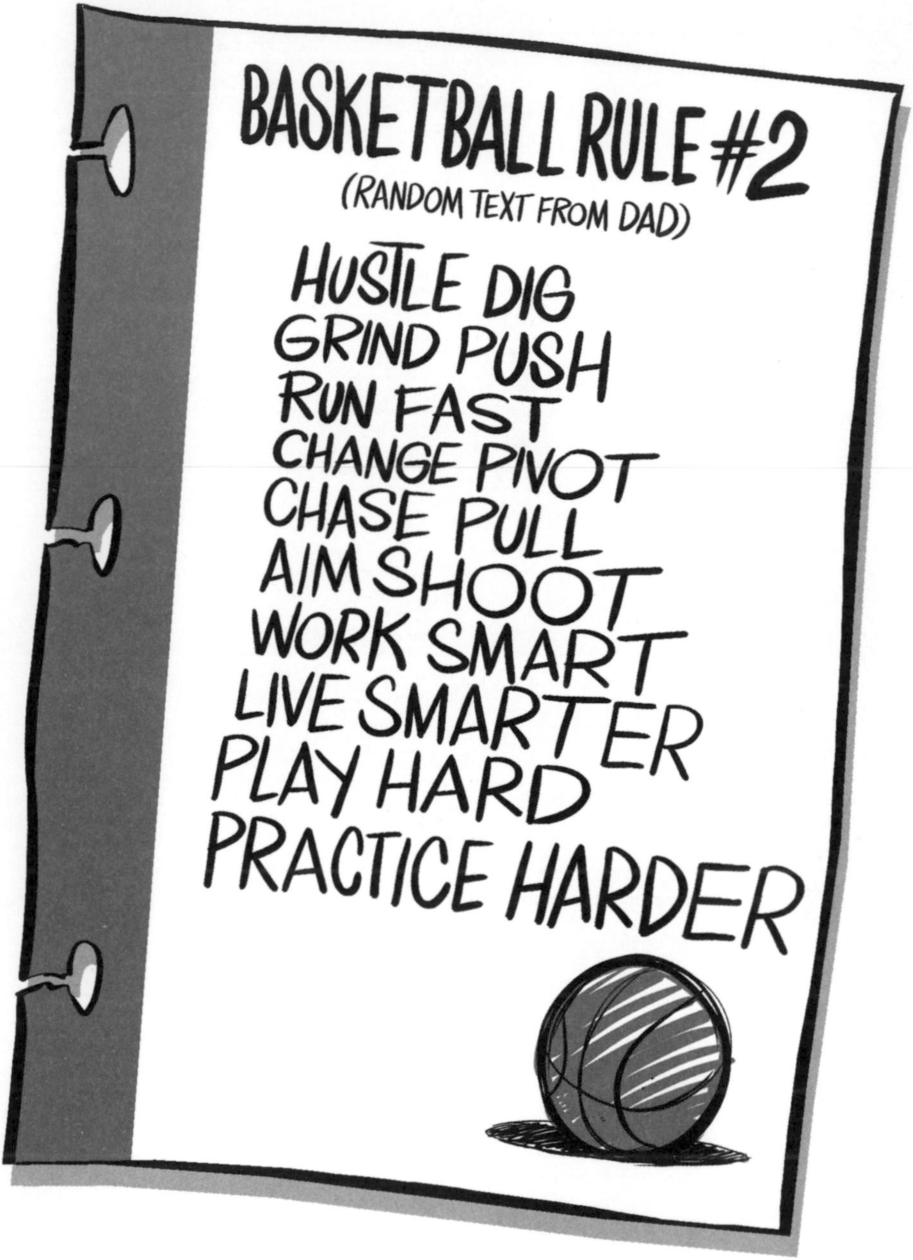
BASKETBALL RULE #2
(RANDOM TEXT FROM DAD)
HUSTLE DIG
GRIND PUSH
RUN FAST
CHANGE PIVOT
CHASE PULL
AIM SHOOT
WORK SMART
LIVE SMARTER
PLAY HARD
PRACTICE HARDER

GIRLS

I WALK INTO THE LUNCHROOM WITH **JB**. HEADS TURN.

I'M NOT BALD LIKE **JB**, BUT MY HAIR'S CLOSE ENOUGH SO THAT PEOPLE SPRINTING PAST US DO DOUBLE-TAKES.

FINALLY, AFTER WE SIT AT OUR TABLE, THE QUESTIONS COME:

WHY'D YOU CUT YOUR HAIR, **FILTHY?**

HOW CAN WE TELL WHO'S **WHO?**

JB ANSWERS, I'M THE COOL ONE WHO MAKES FREE THROWS, AND I **HOLLER,**

I'M THE ONE WHO CAN **DUNK.**

WE **BOTH** GET LAUGHS.

SOME GIRL WHO WE'VE NEVER SEEN BEFORE, IN TIGHT JEANS AND PINK REEBOKS, COMES UP TO THE TABLE.

JB'S EYES ARE OCEAN WIDE, HIS MOUTH SWIMMING ON THE FLOOR, HIS CLOWNISH GRIN, **EMBARRASSING.**

SO WHEN SHE SAYS, IS IT TRUE THAT TWINS KNOW WHAT EACH OTHER ARE THINKING?

I TELL HER YOU DON'T HAVE TO BE HIS **TWIN** TO KNOW WHAT HE'S THINKING.

WHILE VONDIE AND JB

DEBATE WHETHER THE NEW GIRL IS A **KNOCKOUT** OR JUST BEAUTIFUL, A **HOTTIE** OR A **CUTIE**, A **LAY-UP** OR A **DUNK**, I FINISH MY VOCABULARY HOMEWORK— AND MY BROTHER'S VOCABULARY HOMEWORK, WHICH I DON'T MIND SINCE

ENGLISH IS MY FAVORITE SUBJECT AND HE DID THE DISHES FOR ME LAST WEEK.

BUT IT'S HARD TO CONCENTRATE IN THE LUNCHROOM WITH THE GIRLS' STEP TEAM PRACTICING IN ONE CORNER, A RAP GROUP PERFORMING IN THE OTHER, AND **VONDIE** AND **JB** WAXING POETIC ABOUT **LOVE** AND BASKETBALL. SO WHEN THEY ASK, **WHAT DO YOU THINK, FILTHY?** I TELL 'EM SHE'S **PULCHRITUDINOUS.**

PUL·CHRI·TU·DI·NOUS
[PALL-KRE-TOO-DEN-NUS] ADJECTIVE

HAVING GREAT PHYSICAL BEAUTY AND **APPEAL**.

AS IN: EVERY GUY IN THE LUNCHROOM IS TRYING TO FLIRT WITH THE NEW GIRL BECAUSE SHE'S SO **PULCHRITUDINOUS**.

AS IN: I'VE NEVER HAD A GIRLFRIEND, BUT IF I DID, YOU BETTER BELIEVE SHE'D BE **PULCHRITUDINOUS**.

AS IN: WAIT A MINUTE— WHY IS THE **PULCHRITUDINOUS** NEW GIRL NOW TALKING TO **MY BROTHER?**

PRACTICE

COACH READS TO US FROM **THE ART OF WAR**: "A WINNING STRATEGY IS NOT ABOUT PLANNING," HE SAYS.

"IT'S ABOUT QUICK RESPONSES TO CHANGING CONDITIONS."

THEN HE HAS US DO FOOTWORK DRILLS FOLLOWED BY FORTY WIND SPRINTS FROM THE BASELINE TO HALF COURT.

THE WINNER DOESN'T HAVE TO PRACTICE TODAY, COACH SAYS, AND **VONDIE** BLASTS OFF LIKE APOLLO 17, HIS LONG LEGS GIVING HIM AN EDGE. BUT I'M THE QUICKEST GUY ON THE TEAM, SO ON THE LAST LAP I RUN HARD, TAKE THE LEAD BY A FOOT, AND EVEN THOUGH I DON'T PLAN IT, I LET HIM WIN AND GET READY TO PRACTICE HARDER.

WALKING HOME

HEY, JB, YOU THINK WE CAN WIN THE COUNTY CHAMPIONSHIP THIS YEAR?

I DON'T KNOW, MAN.

HEY, JB, WHY DO YOU THINK DAD NEVER HAD KNEE SURGERY?

MAN, I DON'T KNOW.

HEY, JB, WHY CAN'T DAD EAT—

LOOK, FILTHY, WE'LL WIN IF YOU STOP MISSING FREE THROWS. NOBODY LIKES DOCTORS. AND DAD CAN'T EAT FOODS WITH TOO MUCH SALT BECAUSE MOM TOLD HIM HE CAN'T. ANY MORE QUESTIONS?

YEAH, ONE MORE. YOU WANT TO PLAY TO TWENTY-ONE WHEN WE GET HOME?

SURE. YOU GOT TEN DOLLARS? HE ASKS.

63

MAN TO MAN

IN THE DRIVEWAY, I'M **SHAKING** AND **BAKING**.
YOU DON'T WANT NONE OF THIS, I SAY.

I'M ABOUT TO **TAKE** IT **TO** THE **HOLE**. KEEP YOUR EYE ON THE BALL.
I'D **HATE** TO SEE YOU **FALL**.
YOU SHOULDA GONE WITH YOUR **GIRLFRIEND** TO THE **MALL**.
JUST PLAY BALL, **JB** SHOUTS.

OKAY, BUT **WATCH OUT**, MY BROTHER, TARHEEL LOVER.
I'M ABOUT TO GO **UNDERCOVER**.

THEN BRING IT, HE SAYS. AND I DO, ALL THE WAY TO THE TOP.
SO **SMOOOOOOTH**, I MAKE HIM **DROP**.

SO **NASTY**, THE FLOOR SHOULD BE **MOPPED**. BUT BEFORE
I CAN **SHOOT**, MOM MAKES US **STOP**:

JOSH, COME CLEAN YOUR ROOM!

AFTER DINNER

DAD TAKES US TO THE REC TO PRACTICE SHOOTING FREE THROWS WITH ONE HAND WHILE HE STANDS TWO FEET IN FRONT OF US, WAVING FRANTICALLY IN OUR FACES.

IT WILL TEACH YOU FOCUS, HE REMINDS US.

THREE PLAYERS FROM THE LOCAL COLLEGE RECOGNIZE DAD AND ASK HIM FOR AUTOGRAPHS "FOR OUR PARENTS."

DAD CHUCKLES ALONG WITH THEM. **JB** IGNORES THEM.

I CHALLENGE THEM:

IT WON'T BE SO FUNNY WHEN WE SHUT YOU **AMATEURS** DOWN, WILL IT? I SAY.

OHHHH,

THIS YOUNG BOY GOT **HOPS** LIKE HIS OL' MAN? THE TALLEST ONE SAYS.

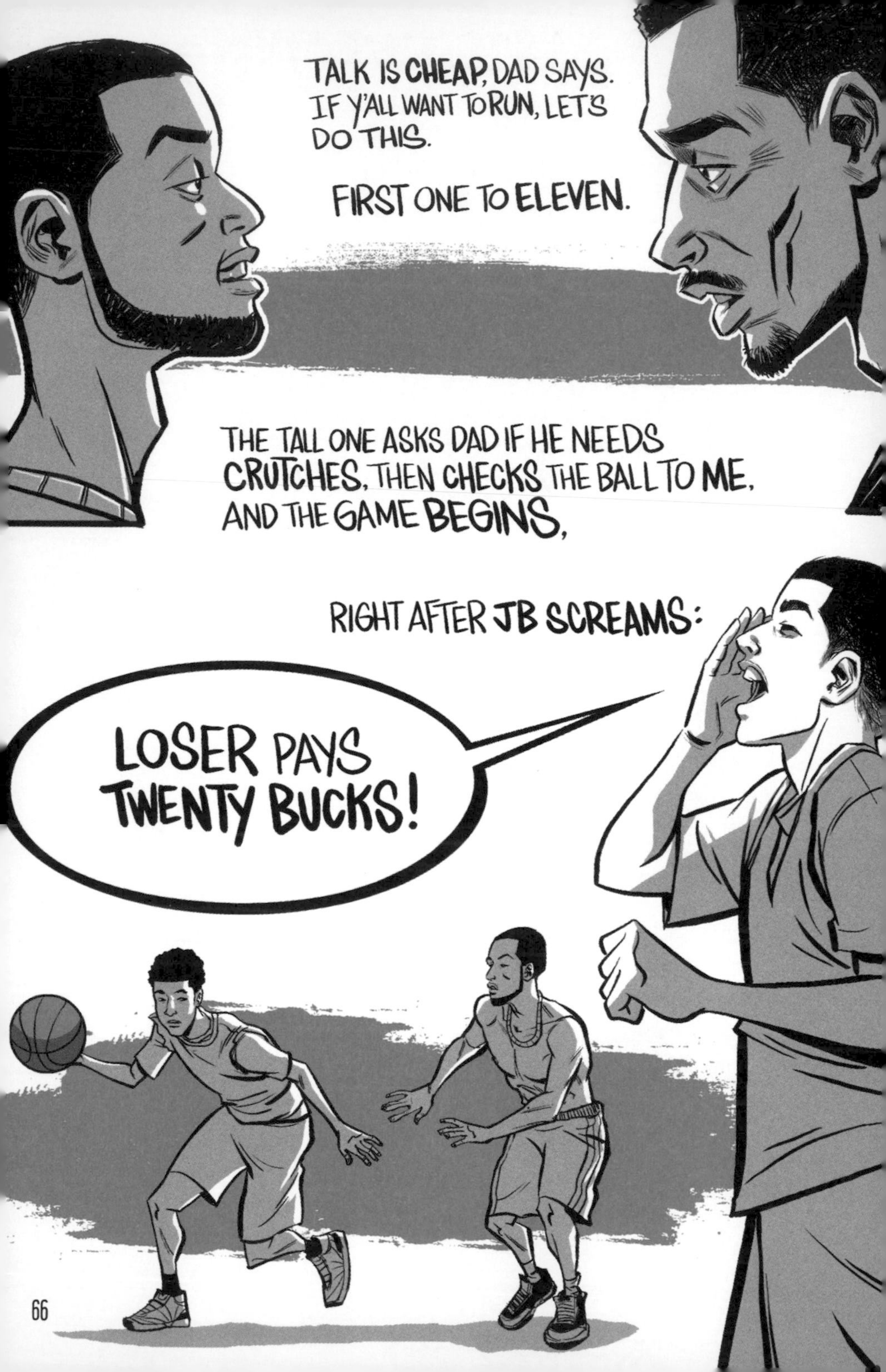
TALK IS CHEAP, DAD SAYS. IF Y'ALL WANT TO RUN, LET'S DO THIS.
FIRST ONE TO ELEVEN.
THE TALL ONE ASKS DAD IF HE NEEDS CRUTCHES, THEN CHECKS THE BALL TO ME, AND THE GAME BEGINS,
RIGHT AFTER JB SCREAMS:
LOSER PAYS TWENTY BUCKS!

AFTER WE WIN

I SEE THE PINK REEBOKS-WEARING GIRL SHOOTING BASKETS ON THE OTHER COURT.

SHE PLAYS BALL, TOO?

JB WALKS OVER TO HER AND I CAN TELL HE LIKES HER BECAUSE WHEN SHE GOES IN FOR A **LAY-UP**, HE DOESN'T **SLAP** THE BALL SILLY LIKE HE TRIES TO DO WITH **ME**.

HE JUST STANDS THERE LOOKING SILLY, SMILING ON THE OTHER COURT AT THE **PINK REEBOKS**-WEARING GIRL.

DAD TAKES US TO KRISPY KREME AND TELLS US HIS FAVORITE STORY (AGAIN)

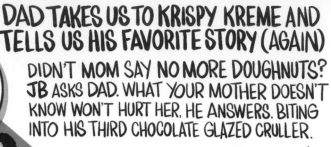

DIDN'T MOM SAY NO MORE DOUGHNUTS? JB ASKS DAD. WHAT YOUR MOTHER DOESN'T KNOW WON'T HURT HER, HE ANSWERS. BITING INTO HIS THIRD CHOCOLATE GLAZED CRULLER.

GOOD SHOOTING TODAY. WE BEAT THOSE BOYS LIKE THEY STOLE SOMETHING, HE ADDS.

WHY DIDN'T WE TAKE THEIR MONEY, DAD? I ASK.

THEY WERE KIDS, **FILTHY**, JUST LIKE Y'ALL. THE LOOK ON THEIR FACES AFTER WE BEAT THEM ELEVEN TO NOTHING WAS ENOUGH FOR ME.

REMEMBER WHEN YOU WERE TWO AND I TAUGHT YOU THE **GAME?**

YOU HAD A BOTTLE IN ONE HAND AND A BALL IN THE OTHER, AND YOUR MOM THOUGHT I WAS **CRAZY.**

I **WAS** CRAZY. CRAZY IN **LOVE.**

WITH MY **TWIN BOYS.**

ONCE, WHEN YOU WERE THREE, I TOOK YOU TO THE PARK TO SHOOT FREE THROWS.

THE GUY WHO WORKED THERE SAID, "THIS BASKET IS TEN FEET TALL. FOR OLDER KIDS. KIDS LIKE YOURS MIGHT AS WELL SHOOT AT THE SUN." AND THEN HE LAUGHED.

AND I ASKED HIM IF A DEAF PERSON COULD WRITE MUSIC.

AND HE SAID, "HUH?" THEN TOOK OUT HIS WRENCH AND TOLD ME, "I'M GONNA LOWER THE GOAL FOR Y'ALL".

WE REMEMBER, DAD.

AND THEN YOU TOLD US BEETHOVEN WAS A FAMOUS MUSICIAN WHO WAS DEAF, AND HOW MANY TIMES DO WE HAVE TO HEAR THE SAME—

AND

DAD INTERRUPTS ME:

INTERRUPT ME AGAIN AND I'LL START ALL OVER.

LIKE I WAS SAYING, I HANDED BOTH OF YOU A **BALL**.

STOOD YOU BETWEEN THE FOUL LINE AND THE **RIM**.

TOLD YOU TO **SHOOT**.

YOU DID.

AND IT WAS **MUSICAL**.

LIKE THE OPENING OF **BEETHOVEN'S FIFTH**.

DA DA DA DUHHHHHHHH.
DA DA DA DUHHHHHHHH.

YOUR SHOTS WHISTLED. LIKE A TRAIN PULLING INTO THE **STATION**.
I EXPECTED YOU TO **MAKE IT**.

AND **YOU DID**.

THE GUY WAS IN **SHOCK**.
HE LOOKED AT ME LIKE
HE'D MISSED THE **TRAIN**.

SWISH

BASKETBALL RULE #3

NEVER LET ANYONE LOWER YOUR GOALS.

OTHERS' EXPECTATIONS OF YOU ARE DETERMINED BY THEIR LIMITATIONS OF LIFE.

THE SKY IS YOUR LIMIT, SONS.

ALWAYS SHOOT FOR THE SUN AND YOU WILL **SHINE**.

JOSH'S PLAY-BY-PLAY

THE RED ROCKETS, DEFENDING COUNTY CHAMPIONS, ARE IN THE HOUSE TONIGHT.

THEY BROUGHT THEIR WHOLE SCHOOL. THIS PLACE IS OOZING CRIMSON

THEY'RE BEATING US TWENTY-NINE TO TWENTY-EIGHT WITH LESS THAN A MINUTE TO GO. I'M AT THE **FREE-THROW** LINE.

ALL I HAVE TO DO IS MAKE BOTH SHOTS TO TAKE THE **LEAD**.

THE FIRST IS UP, **UP**, AND—

—IT HITS THE RIM.

THE SECOND LOOKS...REAL... GOO...**MISSED AGAIN!**

BUT

VONDIE GRABS THE REBOUND, A FRESH **TWENTY-FOUR** ON THE SHOT CLOCK. NUMBER THIRTY-THREE ON THE **ROCKETS** STRIPS THE **BALL** FROM **VONDIE**.

THIS GAME IS LIKE **PING-PONG**, WITH ALL THE BACK-AND-FORTH.

HE RACES DOWNCOURT FOR AN **EASY LAY—**

OHHHHHHH! HOUSTON, WE HAVE A **PROBLEM!** I CATCH HIM AND SLAP THE BALL ON THE GLASS. EVER SEEN ANYTHING LIKE THIS FROM A SEVENTH-GRADER?

DIDN'T THINK SO! ME AND **JB** ARE STARS IN THE MAKING. THE **ROCKETS** FULL-COURT-PRESS ME. BUT I GET IT ACROSS THE LINE JUST IN TIME.

TEN SECONDS LEFT. I PASS THE BALL TO **JB.** THEY DOUBLE-TEAM HIM IN A HURRY—DON'T WANT TO GIVE HIM AN EASY **THREE.**

FIVE SECONDS LEFT. **JB LOBS** THE BALL, I RISE LIKE A **LEARJET**— SEVENTH-GRADERS AREN'T SUPPOSED TO **DUNK.**

BUT GUESS **WHAT?**

I SNATCH THE BALL OUT OF THE AIR AND **SLAM!**

YAM! IN YOUR **MUG!**

WHO'S DA MAN?

LET'S LOOK AT THAT AGAIN.

OH, I FORGOT, THIS IS JUNIOR HIGH. NO INSTANT REPLAY UNTIL COLLEGE.

WELL, WITH GAME LIKE THIS THAT'S WHERE ME AND JB ARE **HEADED.**

SLAM!

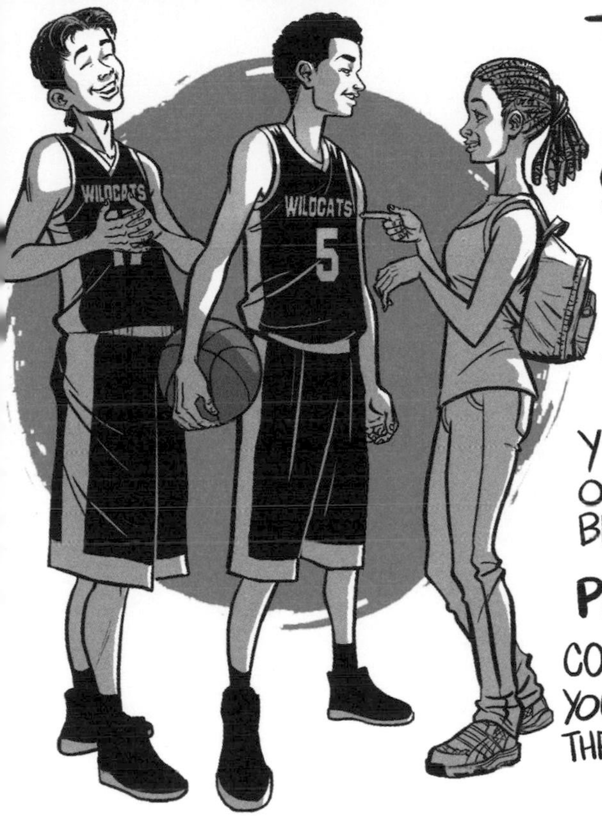

WILDCATS
WILDCATS
5

THE NEW GIRL

COMES UP TO ME AFTER THE GAME, HER SMILE OCEAN WIDE, MY MOUTH WIDE SHUT.

NICE DUNK, SHE SAYS.
THANKS.

Y'ALL COMING TO THE GYM OVER THE **THANKSGIVING** BREAK?

PROBABLY!

COOL. BY THE WAY, WHY'D YOU CUT YOUR **LOCKS**? THEY WERE KIND OF **CUTE**.

STANDING RIGHT BEHIND ME, **VONDIE** GIGGLES.

KIND OF CUTE, HE **MOCKS**.

THEN **JB** WALKS UP.

HEY, **JB**, GREAT GAME. I BROUGHT YOU SOME ICED TEA, SHE SAYS.

IS IT **SWEET**? HE ASKS.

AND JUST LIKE THAT **JB** AND THE NEW GIRL ARE **SIPPING SWEET TEA TOGETHER**.

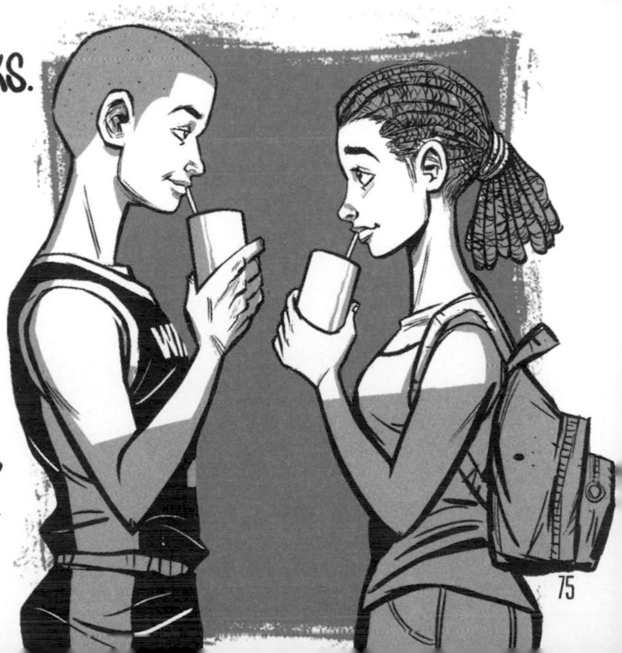

I MISSED THREE FREE THROWS TONIGHT

EACH NIGHT AFTER DINNER DAD MAKES US SHOOT FREE THROWS UNTIL WE MAKE TEN IN A ROW.

TONIGHT HE SAYS I HAVE TO MAKE FIFTEEN.

BASKETBALL
RULE #4

IF YOU MISS ENOUGH OF LIFE'S FREE THROWS, YOU WILL PAY IN THE END.

HAVING A MOTHER

IS GOOD WHEN SHE RESCUES YOU FROM FREE-THROW ATTEMPT NUMBER THIRTY-SIX, YOUR ARMS AS HEAVY AS SEA ANCHORS.

BUT IT CAN BE BAD WHEN YOUR MOTHER IS A PRINCIPAL AT YOUR SCHOOL. BAD IN SO MANY WAYS. IT'S ALWAYS EDUCATION THIS AND EDUCATION THAT.

AFTER A DOUBLE-OVERTIME BASKETBALL GAME I ONLY WANT THREE THINGS: FOOD, BATH, SLEEP. THE LAST THING I WANT IS **EDUCATION!**

BUT, EACH NIGHT, MOM MAKES US READ. DON'T KNOW HOW HE DOES IT, BUT **JB** LISTENS TO HIS iPOD AT THE SAME TIME, SO HE DOESN'T HEAR ME WHEN I ASK HIM IS **MISS SWEET TEA** HIS GIRLFRIEND.

HE CLAIMS HE'S LISTENING TO **FRENCH CLASSICAL**, THAT IT HELPS HIM CONCENTRATE. YEAH, RIGHT! SOUNDS MORE LIKE **JAY-Z** AND **KANYE** IN **PARIS**. WHICH IS WHY WHEN MOM AND DAD START ARGUING, HE DOESN'T HEAR THEM, EITHER.

MOM SHOUTS

GET A CHECKUP. HYPERTENSION IS GENETIC.

I'M FINE, STOP HIGH-POSTING ME, BABY, DAD WHISPERS.

DON'T PLAY ME, CHARLES—THIS ISN'T A BASKETBALL GAME.

I DON'T NEED A DOCTOR, I'M FINE.

YOUR FATHER DIDN'T "NEED" A DOCTOR EITHER.

HE WAS ALIVE WHEN HE WENT INTO THE HOSPITAL.

SO NOW YOU'RE AFRAID OF HOSPITALS?
NOBODY'S AFRAID. I'M FINE. IT'S NOT THAT SERIOUS.

FAINTING IS A JOKE, IS IT?
I SAW YOU, BABY, AND I GOT A LITTLE EXCITED. COME KISS ME.

DON'T DO THAT...
BABY, IT'S NOTHING. I JUST GOT A LITTLE DIZZY.

YOU LOVE ME?
LIKE SUMMER LOVES SHORT NIGHTS.

GET A CHECKUP, THEN.
ONLY CURE I NEED IS YOU.

I'M SERIOUS ABOUT THIS, CHUCK. ONLY DOCTOR I NEED IS DR. CRYSTAL BELL. NOW COME HERE...

AND THEN THERE IS SILENCE, SO I PUT THE PILLOW OVER MY HEAD BECAUSE WHEN THEY STOP TALKING,

I KNOW WHAT THAT MEANS.

UGGGHH!

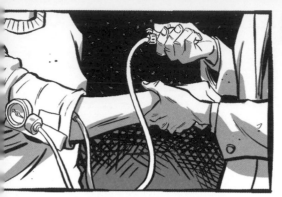

HY·PER·TEN·SION
[HI-PER-TEN-SHUHN] NOUN

A DISEASE OTHERWISE KNOWN AS **HIGH BLOOD PRESSURE.**

AS IN: MOM DOESN'T WANT DAD EATING **SALT,** BECAUSE TOO MUCH OF IT INCREASES THE VOLUME OF **BLOOD,** WHICH CAN CAUSE **HYPERTENSION.**

AS IN: **HYPERTENSION** CAN AFFECT ALL TYPES OF PEOPLE, BUT YOU HAVE A **HIGHER RISK** IF SOMEONE IN YOUR FAMILY HAS HAD THE **DISEASE.**

AS IN: I THINK MY GRANDFATHER DIED OF **HYPERTENSION?**

TO FALL ASLEEP

I COUNT AND RECOUNT THE **THIRTY-SEVEN** STRANDS OF MY PAST IN THE BOX BENEATH MY BED.

WHY WE ONLY ATE SALAD FOR THANKSGIVING

BECAUSE EVERY YEAR GRANDMA MAKES A BIG DELICIOUS DINNER BUT THIS YEAR TWO DAYS BEFORE THANKSGIVING SHE FELL OFF HER FRONT STOOP ON THE WAY TO BUY GROCERIES

SO UNCLE BOB, MY MOM'S YOUNGER BROTHER (WHO SMOKES CIGARS AND THINKS HE'S A CHEF BECAUSE HE WATCHES **FOOD TV**), DECIDED HE WOULD PREPARE A FEAST FOR THE WHOLE FAMILY WHICH CONSISTED OF MACARONI WITH NO CHEESE CONCRETE-HARD CORNBREAD AND A GREENISH-LOOKING HAM THAT PROMPTED MOM

TO ASK IF HE HAD ANY EGGS TO GO ALONG WITH IT WHICH MADE GRANDMA LAUGH SO HARD SHE FELL AGAIN, THIS TIME RIGHT OUT OF HER **WHEELCHAIR.**

HOW DO YOU SPELL TROUBLE?

DURING THE VOCABULARY TEST **JB** PASSES ME A FOLDED NOTE TO GIVE TO **MISS SWEET TEA**, WHO SITS AT THE DESK IN FRONT OF ME AND WHO LOOKS PRETTY TIGHT IN HER **PINK DENIM CAPRIS** AND MATCHING **SNEAKS**.

SOMEONE CRACKS A WINDOW. A COLD BREEZE **WHISTLES**. HER HAIR DANCES TO ITS **OWN SONG**.

PAP!

IN THIS MOMENT I FORGET ABOUT THE TEST AND THE NOTE UNTIL **JB** HITS ME IN THE **HEAD** WITH HIS **NO. 2**.

SOMEWHERE BETWEEN **CAMARADERIE** AND **IMBECILE** I TAP HER BEIGE BARE SHOULDER.

AT THAT EXACT MOMENT THE TEACHER'S HEAD CREEPS UP FROM HIS DESK, HIS EYES DIRECTLY ON ME.

I'M A FLY CAUGHT IN A WEB. WHAT DO I DO?

HAND OVER THE NOTE, EMBARRASS JB; OR HIDE THE NOTE, TAKE THE **HEAT**.

I LOOK AT MY BROTHER, HIS FOREHEAD A FACTORY OF SWEAT.

MISS SWEET TEA SMILES, GORGEOUS PINK LIPS AND ALL.

I KNOW WHAT I HAVE TO DO.

BAD NEWS

I SIT IN MOM'S OFFICE FOR AN **HOUR**, READING BROCHURES AND **PAMPHLETS** ABOUT THE **AIR FORCE** AND THE **MARINES**.

SHE'S IN AND OUT **HANDLING** PRINCIPAL STUFF:

A PARENT PROTESTING HER DAUGHTER'S **F**;

A PRANKED SUBSTITUTE TEACHER **CRYING**;

A **BROKEN WINDOW**.

AFTER AN HOUR SHE FINALLY SITS IN THE CHAIR NEXT TO ME AND SAYS, THE **GOOD NEWS** IS, I'M NOT GOING TO **SUSPEND** YOU.

THE **BAD NEWS, JOSH,** IS THAT NEITHER **DUKE** NOR ANY OTHER COLLEGE ACCEPTS **CHEATERS**.

SINCE I CAN'T SEEM TO MAKE A DECENT MAN OUT OF YOU, PERHAPS THE **AIR FORCE** OR **MARINES** CAN.

I WANT TO TELL HER I WASN'T CHEATING, THAT THIS IS ALL **JB** AND **MISS SWEET TEA'S** FAULT, THAT THIS WILL **NEVER HAPPEN AGAIN**, THAT **DUKE** IS THE **ONLY** THING THAT MATTERS, BUT A WATER PIPE **BURSTS** IN THE GIRLS' BATHROOM.

SO I TELL HER I'M SORRY, IT WON'T HAPPEN AGAIN, THEN HEAD OFF TO MY NEXT CLASS.

GYM CLASS

IS SUPPOSED TO BE ABOUT BALLS: VOLLEYBALLS, BASKETBALLS, SOFTBALLS, SOCCER BALLS— SOMETIMES SIT-UPS AND ALWAYS **SWEAT**.

BUT TODAY **MR. LANE'S** STANDING IN FRONT OF THE CLASS, A **DUMMY** LAID OUT ON THE FLOOR, PLASTIC, ARMLESS, TORSO CUT IN **HALF**.

I'M **NOT** PAYING ATTENTION TO ANYTHING HE'S SAYING OR TO THE **DUMMY** BECAUSE

I'M WATCHING JORDAN PASS NOTES TO MISS SWEET TEA. AND I WONDER WHAT'S IN THE NOTES.
JOSH, WHY DON'T YOU COME UP AND ASSIST ME.
WHAT? HUH?
THE CLASS SNICKERS, AND BEFORE I KNOW IT

I'M TILTING THE DUMMY'S HEAD BACK, PINCHING HIS NOSE, BLOWING IN HIS MOUTH,
5
AND PUMPING HIS CHEST THIRTY TIMES.
ALL THE WHILE THINKING THAT IF LIFE IS REALLY FAIR
ONE DAY I'LL BE THE ONE WRITING NOTES TO SOME SWEET GIRL AND JB WILL HAVE TO SQUASH HIS LIPS ON SOME DUMMY'S SWEATY MOUTH.

SECOND QUARTER

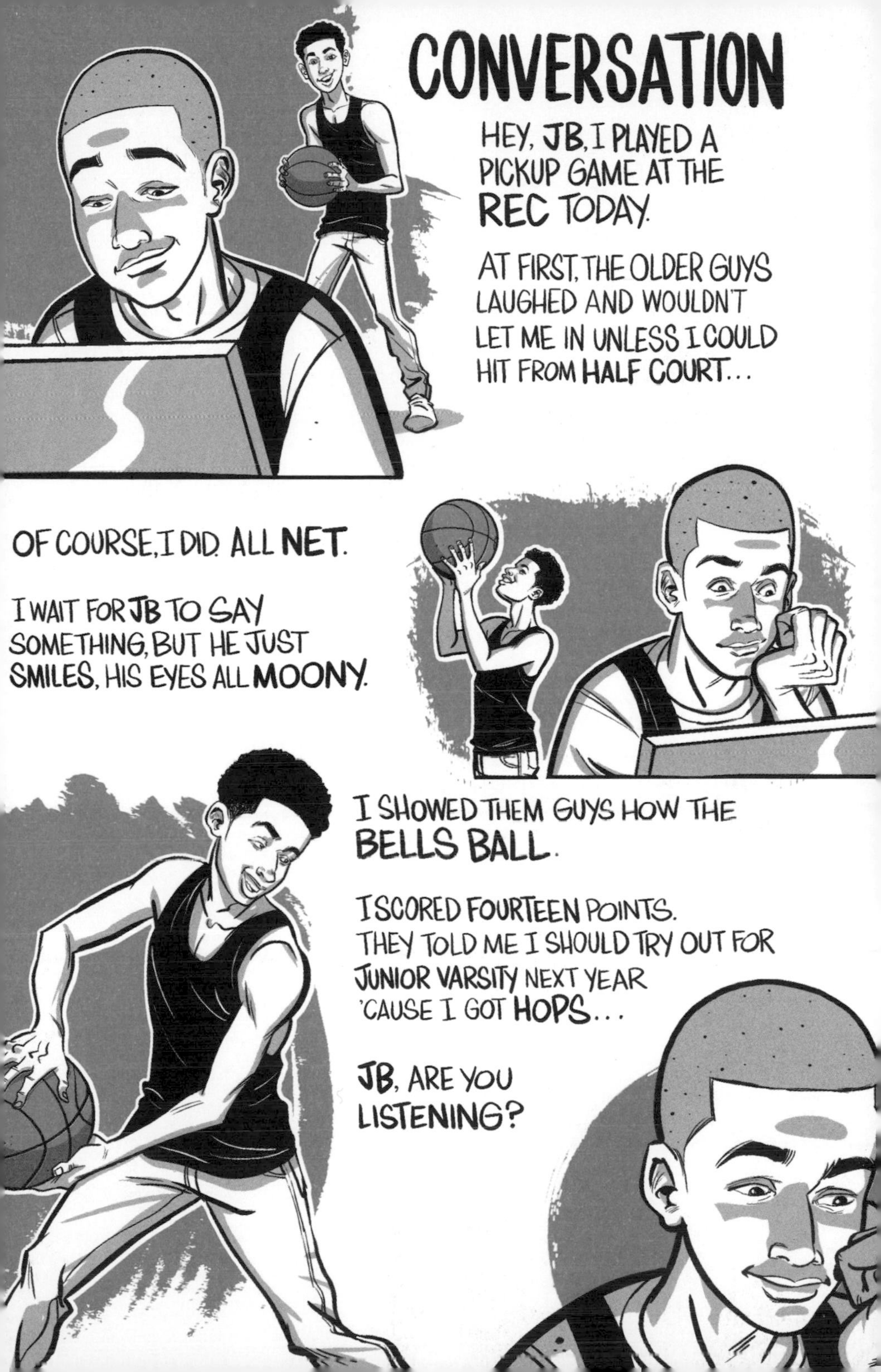
CONVERSATION
HEY, JB, I PLAYED A PICKUP GAME AT THE REC TODAY.
AT FIRST, THE OLDER GUYS LAUGHED AND WOULDN'T LET ME IN UNLESS I COULD HIT FROM HALF COURT...
OF COURSE, I DID. ALL NET.
I WAIT FOR JB TO SAY SOMETHING, BUT HE JUST SMILES, HIS EYES ALL MOONY.
I SHOWED THEM GUYS HOW THE BELLS BALL.
I SCORED FOURTEEN POINTS. THEY TOLD ME I SHOULD TRY OUT FOR JUNIOR VARSITY NEXT YEAR 'CAUSE I GOT HOPS...
JB, ARE YOU LISTENING?

JB NODS, HIS FINGERS TAPPING AWAY ON THE COMPUTER, CHATTING PROBABLY WITH MISS SWEET TEA.

I TOLD THE BIG GUYS ABOUT YOU, TOO. THEY SAID WE COULD COME BACK AND RUN WITH THEM ANYTIME.

WHAT DO YOU THINK ABOUT THAT?

HELLO—EARTH TO JB?

EVEN THOUGH I KNOW HE HEARS ME, THE ONLY THING JB IS LISTENING TO IS THE SOUND OF HIS HEART BOUNCING ON THE COURT OF LOVE.

CONVERSATION

DAD, THIS GIRL IS MAKING JORDAN ACT WEIRD.

HE'S HERE, BUT HE'S NOT. HE'S ALWAYS SMILING. HIS EYES GET ALL SPACEY WHENEVER SHE'S AROUND, AND SOMETIMES WHEN SHE'S NOT.

HE WEARS YOUR COLOGNE. HE'S ALWAYS TEXTING HER. HE EVEN WORE LOAFERS TO SCHOOL.

DAD, YOU GOTTA DO SOMETHING.

DAD DOES DO SOMETHING.

HE LAUGHS.

FILTHY, TALKING TO YOUR BROTHER RIGHT NOW WOULD BE LIKE PUSHING WATER UPHILL WITH A RAKE, SON.

THIS ISN'T FUNNY, DAD. SAY SOMETHING TO HIM. PLEASE.

FILTHY, IF SOME GIRL DONE LOCKED UP JB, HE'S GOING TO JAIL.

NOW LET'S GO GET SOME DOUGHNUTS.

BASKETBALL RULE #5

WHEN YOU STOP PLAYING YOUR GAME YOU'VE ALREADY LOST.

SHOWOFF

UP BY SIXTEEN WITH SIX SECONDS
SHOWING, JB SMILES, THEN
STRUTS, SIDE STEPS, STUTTERS,
SPINS, AND SINKS

A SICK SLICK SLIDING

sWeeeeeeeeeeT

SEVEN-FOOT SHOT.

WHAT A
SHOWOFF.

95

OUT OF CONTROL

ARE YOU KIDDING ME?

COME ON. REF, OPEN YOUR EYES. RAY CHARLES COULD HAVE SEEN THAT KID WALKED.

CALL THE TRAVELING VIOLATION! YOU GUYS ARE TERRIBLE!

MOM WASN'T AT THE GAME TONIGHT, WHICH MEANT THAT ALL NIGHT DAD WAS FREE TO YELL AT THE OFFICIALS, WHICH HE DID.

MOM CALLS ME INTO THE KITCHEN

AFTER WE GET HOME FROM BEATING ST. FRANCIS. NORMALLY SHE WANTS ME TO SAMPLE THE MACARONI AND CHEESE TO MAKE SURE IT'S CHEESY ENOUGH, OR THE OVEN-BAKED FRIED CHICKEN TO MAKE SURE IT'S NOT GREASY AND STUFF, BUT TODAY ON THE TABLE IS SOME GROSS-LOOKING ORANGE CREAMY DIP WITH BROWN SPECKS IN IT.

A TRAY OF **PITA-BREAD** TRIANGLES IS BESIDE IT. MAYBE **MOM** IS HAVING ONE OF HER BOOK CLUB MEETINGS.

SIT DOWN, SHE SAYS. I SIT AS FAR AWAY FROM THE DIP AS POSSIBLE. **MAYBE THE CHICKEN** IS IN THE **OVEN**. WHERE IS YOUR **BROTHER?** SHE ASKS.

PROBABLY ON THE PHONE WITH THAT GIRL.

SHE HANDS ME A **PITA**.

NO THANKS, I SAY, THEN STAND UP TO LEAVE, BUT SHE GIVES ME A LOOK THAT TELLS ME SHE'S NOT FINISHED WITH ME.

MAYBE THE **MAC** IS IN THE **OVEN**.

WE'VE TALKED TO YOU TWO ABOUT
YOUR GRANDFATHER, SHE SAYS.

HE WAS A GOOD MAN. I'M SORRY
YOU NEVER GOT TO MEET HIM, JOSH.
ME TOO, HE LOOKED COOL IN HIS
UNIFORMS.

THAT MAN WAS WAY PAST COOL.
DAD SAID HE USED TO CURSE
A LOT AND TALK ABOUT THE WAR.
MOM'S LAUGH IS SHORT, THEN
SHE'S SERIOUS AGAIN.

I KNOW WE TOLD YOU
GRANDPOP DIED AFTER A FALL,
BUT THE TRUTH IS HE FELL
BECAUSE HE HAD A STROKE.

HE HAD A HEART DISEASE.

TOO MANY YEARS OF BAD
EATING AND NOT TAKING
CARE OF HIMSELF AND SO—

WHAT DOES THIS HAVE TO DO WITH
ANYTHING? I ASK, EVEN THOUGH I
THINK I ALREADY KNOW.

WELL, OUR FAMILY HAS A HISTORY OF
HEART PROBLEMS, SHE SAYS, SO WE'RE
GOING TO START EATING BETTER.
ESPECIALLY DAD.

AND WE'RE GOING TO START TONIGHT WITH
SOME HUMMUS AND PITA BREAD.

FOR MY VICTORY DINNER?
JOSH, WE'RE GOING TO TRY TO LAY OFF THE FRIED FOODS AND GOLDEN DRAGON.
AND WHEN YOUR DAD TAKES YOU TO THE RECREATION CENTER, NO POLLARD'S OR KRISPY KREME AFTERWARD, UNDERSTAND?

AND I UNDERSTAND MORE THAN SHE THINKS I DO.
BUT IS HUMMUS REALLY THE ANSWER?

35-18

IS THE FINAL SCORE OF GAME SIX. A LOCAL REPORTER ASKS JB AND I HOW WE GOT SO GOOD.

DAD SCREAMS FROM BEHIND US, THEY LEARNED FROM

Da Man!

THE CROWD OF PARENTS AND STUDENTS BEHIND US LAUGHS.

ON THE WAY HOME DAD ASKS IF WE SHOULD STOP AT **POLLARD'S**.

I TELL HIM I'M NOT HUNGRY, PLUS I HAVE A LOT OF **HOMEWORK**, EVEN THOUGH I **SKIPPED** LUNCH TODAY AND FINISHED MY **HOMEWORK** DURING **HALFTIME**.

TOO GOOD

LATELY, I'VE BEEN FEELING LIKE EVERYTHING IN MY LIFE IS GOING RIGHT:

I BEAT **JB** IN **MADDEN.**
OUR TEAM IS **UNDEFEATED.**

I SCORED AN **A+** ON THE
VOCABULARY TEST.

PLUS, MOM'S AWAY AT A
CONFERENCE, WHICH MEANS SO
IS THE **ASSISTANT PRINCIPAL.**

Name: Josh Bell
OCABULARY TEST
A+

I AM A LITTLE WORRIED, THOUGH, BECAUSE, AS COACH LIKES TO SAY, YOU CAN GET USED TO THINGS GOING WELL, BUT YOU'RE NEVER PREPARED FOR SOMETHING GOING WRONG.

I'M ON FREE THROW NUMBER TWENTY-SEVEN

WE TAKE TURNS, SWITCHING EVERY TIME WE MISS. JB HAS HIT FORTY-ONE, THE LAST TWELVE IN A ROW. FILTHY, KEEP UP, MAN, KEEP UP, HE SAYS. DAD LAUGHS LOUD AND SAYS,

FILTHY, YOUR BROTHER IS PUTTING ON A FREE-THROW CLINIC.

YOU BETTER—

AND SUDDENLY HE BOWLS OVER,

A LOOK OF **HORROR** ON HIS FACE, AND STARTS **COUGHING** WHILE **CLUTCHING** HIS CHEST,

ONLY NO SOUND COMES.

I FREEZE.

JB RUNS OVER TO HIM.

DAD, YOU OKAY?
HE ASKS.

I STILL CAN'T MOVE.

THERE IS A STREAM OF SWEAT ON DAD'S FACE. MAYBE HE'S OVERHEATING, I SAY.

HIS MOUTH IS CURLED UP LIKE A LITTLE **TUNNEL**.

JB GRABS THE WATER HOSE, TURNS THE FAUCET ON FULL BLAST, AND SPRAYS DAD.

SOME OF IT GOES IN DAD'S MOUTH.

THEN I HEAR THE SOUND OF COUGHING, AND DAD IS NO LONGER LEANING AGAINST THE CAR,

NOW HE'S MOVING TOWARD THE HOSE, AND LAUGHING.

SO IS JB.

THEN DAD GRABS THE HOSE

AND SPRAYS BOTH OF US.

NOW I'M **LAUGHING** TOO, BUT ONLY ON THE OUTSIDE.

HE PROBABLY

JUST GOT SOMETHING STUCK IN HIS THROAT, **JB** SAYS WHEN I ASK HIM IF HE THOUGHT DAD WAS SICK AND SHOULDN'T WE TELL MOM WHAT HAPPENED.

SO, WHEN THE PHONE RINGS, IT'S **IRONIC** THAT AFTER SAYING HELLO, HE **THROWS** THE PHONE TO ME, BECAUSE, EVEN THOUGH HIS LIPS ARE **MOVING, JB** IS **SPEECHLESS**, LIKE HE'S GOT SOMETHING **STUCK** IN HIS **THROAT.**

I·RON·IC
[AY-RON-IK] ADJECTIVE

HAVING A CURIOUS OR **HUMOROUS** UNEXPECTED SEQUENCE OF EVENTS MARKED BY COINCIDENCE.

AS IN: THE FACT THAT **VONDIE** HATES **ASTRONOMY** AND HIS MOM WORKS FOR **NASA** IS **IRONIC.**

AS IN: IT'S NOT **IRONIC** THAT GRANDPOP DIED IN A HOSPITAL AND DAD DOESN'T LIKE **DOCTORS.**

AS IN: ISN'T IT **IRONIC** THAT SHOWOFF **JB**, WITH ALL HIS **SWAGGER**, IS TOO SHY TO TALK TO **MISS SWEET TEA**, SO HE GIVES ME THE PHONE?

THIS IS ALEXIS— MAY I PLEASE SPEAK TO JORDAN?

IDENTICAL TWINS ARE NO DIFFERENT FROM EVERYONE ELSE, EXCEPT WE LOOK AND SOMETIMES SOUND EXACTLY ALIKE.

PHONE CONVERSATION (I SUB FOR JB)

WAS THAT YOUR BROTHER?
YEP, THAT WAS JOSH. I'M JB.

**I KNOW WHO YOU ARE,
SILLY — I CALLED YOU.**
UH, RIGHT. YOU HAVE ANY
SIBLINGS, ALEXIS?

**TWO SISTERS. I'M THE
YOUNGEST.**
AND THE PRETTIEST.

YOU HAVEN'T SEEN THEM.
I DON'T NEED TO.

THAT'S SWEET.
SWEET AS POMEGRANATE.

OKAY, THAT WAS RANDOM.
THAT'S ME.

**JORDAN, CAN I ASK YOU
SOMETHING?**
YEP.

DID YOU GET MY TEXT?
UH, YEAH.

SO, WHAT'S YOUR ANSWER?
UH, MY ANSWER. I DON'T KNOW.

STOP BEING SILLY, JORDAN.
I'M NOT.

THEN TELL ME YOUR
ANSWER. ARE Y'ALL RICH?
I DON'T KNOW.

DIDN'T YOUR DAD PLAY IN
THE NBA?
NO, HE PLAYED IN ITALY.

BUT STILL, HE MADE A LOT
OF MONEY, RIGHT?
IT'S NOT LIKE WE'RE OPULENT.

WHO SAYS "OPULENT"?
I DO.

YOU NEVER USE BIG WORDS LIKE THAT AT SCHOOL...
I HAVE A REPUTATION TO UPHOLD.

IS HE COOL?
WHO?

YOUR DAD.
VERY.

SO, WHEN ARE YOU GONNA
INTRODUCE ME?
INTRODUCE YOU?

TO YOUR PARENTS.
I'M WAITING FOR THE RIGHT
MOMENT.

WHICH IS WHEN?
UH—

SO, AM I YOUR GIRLFRIEND
OR NOT?
UH, CAN YOU HOLD ON FOR A
SECOND?

SURE, SHE SAYS.

COVER THE MOUTHPIECE, JB
MOUTHS TO ME. I DO, THEN
WHISPER TO HIM:
SHE WANTS TO KNOW ARE YOU
HER BOYFRIEND.

AND WHEN ARE YOU GONNA
INTRODUCE HER TO MOM AND
DAD. WHAT SHOULD I TELL
HER, JB?

TELL HER YEAH,
I GUESS, I MEAN,
I DON'T KNOW.

I GOTTA PEE, JB SAYS,
RUNNING OUT OF THE
ROOM, LEAVING ME STILL
IN HIS SHOES.

OKAY, I'M BACK, ALEXIS.
SO, WHAT'S THE VERDICT,
JORDAN?

DO YOU WANT TO BE MY
GIRLFRIEND?
ARE YOU ASKING ME TO BE
YOUR GIRL?

UH, I THINK SO.
YOU THINK SO? WELL, I HAVE
TO GO NOW.

YES.
YES, WHAT?

I LIKE YOU. A LOT.
I LIKE YOU, TOO . . . PRECIOUS.

SO, NOW I'M PRECIOUS?
EVERYONE CALLS YOU JB.

THEN I GUESS IT'S OFFICIAL.
TEXT ME LATER.

GOOD NIGHT, MISS SWEET—
WHAT DID YOU CALL ME?

UH, GOOD NIGHT, MY SWEETNESS.
GOOD NIGHT, PRECIOUS.

JB COMES RUNNING OUT OF THE BATHROOM.
WHAT'D SHE SAY, JOSH?

COME ON, TELL ME.

SHE SAID SHE LIKES ME A LOT, I TELL
HIM.

YOU MEAN SHE LIKES ME A LOT?
HE ASKS.

YEAH . . . THAT'S WHAT I MEANT.

JB AND I

EAT LUNCH TOGETHER EVERY DAY, TAKING BITES OF MOM'S **TUNA SALAD** ON WHEAT BETWEEN ARGUMENTS:

WHO'S THE BETTER DUNKER,

BLAKE OR **LeBRON?**

WHICH IS SUPERIOR, **NIKE**

OR **CONVERSE?**

ONLY TODAY I WAIT AT OUR TABLE IN THE BACK FOR TWENTY-FIVE MINUTES, TEXTING **VONDIE** (HOME SICK), EATING A **FRUIT CUP** (ALONE), BEFORE I SEE **JB** STRUT INTO THE **CAFETERIA** WITH **MISS SWEET TEA** HOLDING HIS **PRECIOUS HAND.**

BOY WALKS INTO A ROOM

WITH A GIRL. THEY COME OVER.
HE SAYS, HEY, FILTHY MCNASTY
LIKE HE'S SAID FOREVER, BUT IT
SOUNDS DIFFERENT THIS TIME, AND
WHEN HE SNICKERS, SHE DOES TOO,
LIKE IT'S SOME INSIDE JOKE,

AND MY NICKNAME,
SOME DIRTY
PUNCH LINE.

AT PRACTICE

COACH SAYS WE NEED TO WORK ON OUR MENTAL GAME. IF WE THINK WE CAN BEAT INDEPENDENCE JUNIOR HIGH—THE DEFENDING CHAMPIONS, THE NUMBER ONE SEED, THE ONLY OTHER UNDEFEATED TEAM— THEN WE WILL.

BUT INSTEAD OF DRILLS AND SPRINTS, WE SIT ON OUR BUTTS, MAKE WEIRD SOUNDS—

OHMMMMMMMM OHMMMMMMMM—

AND **MEDITATE**.

SUDDENLY I GET THIS **VISION** OF JB IN A **HOSPITAL**.

I QUICKLY OPEN MY EYES, TURN AROUND, AND SEE HIM LOOKING DEAD AT ME LIKE HE'S JUST SEEN A GHOST.

SECOND-PERSON

AFTER PRACTICE, YOU WALK HOME ALONE.

THIS FEELS STRANGE TO YOU, BECAUSE AS LONG AS YOU CAN REMEMBER THERE HAS ALWAYS BEEN A SECOND PERSON.

ON TODAY'S LONG, HOT MILE, YOU BOUNCE YOUR BASKETBALL, BUT YOUR MIND IS ON SOMETHING ELSE.

NOT WHETHER YOU WILL MAKE THE **PLAYOFFS**.

NOT **HOMEWORK**.

NOT EVEN WHAT'S FOR **DINNER**.

YOU WONDER WHAT **JB** AND HIS **PINK REEBOKS**-WEARING
GIRLFRIEND ARE DOING.

YOU DO NOT WANT TO GO TO THE **LIBRARY.**

BUT YOU **GO.** BECAUSE YOUR REPORT ON **THE GIVER** IS DUE
TOMORROW. AND **JB** HAS YOUR COPY.

BUT HE'S WITH **HER.** NOT HERE WITH **YOU.**

WHICH IS **UNFAIR.**

BECAUSE HE DOESN'T ARGUE WITH YOU ABOUT WHO'S THE GREATEST,
MICHAEL JORDAN OR **BILL RUSSELL,** LIKE HE USED TO.

BECAUSE **JB** WILL NOT EAT LUNCH WITH YOU TOMORROW OR THE
NEXT DAY, OR **NEXT WEEK.**

BECAUSE YOU ARE WALKING HOME BY YOURSELF
AND YOUR **BROTHER** OWNS THE **WORLD.**

THIRD WHEEL

YOU WALK INTO THE LIBRARY, GLANCE OVER AT THE MUSIC SECTION.

YOU LOOK THROUGH THE MAGAZINES.

YOU EVEN SIT AT A DESK AND PRETEND TO STUDY.

YOU ASK THE LIBRARIAN WHERE YOU CAN FIND **THE GIVER**.

SHE SAYS SOMETHING ODD: DID YOU FIND YOUR FRIEND?

THEN SHE POINTS UPSTAIRS.

ON THE SECOND FLOOR, YOU PASS BY THE **COMPUTERS**.

KIDS CHECKING THEIR **FACEBOOK**.

MORE KIDS IN LINE WAITING TO CHECK THEIR **FACEBOOK**.

IN THE **BIOGRAPHY** SECTION YOU SEE AN OLD MAN READING THE **TIPPING POINT**.

YOU WALK DOWN THE LAST AISLE, TEEN FICTION, AND COME TO THE REASON YOU'RE HERE.

YOU REMOVE THE BOOK FROM THE SHELF.

AND THERE, BEHIND THE LAST ROW OF BOOKS, YOU FIND THE "FRIEND" THE LIBRARIAN WAS TALKING ABOUT.

ONLY SHE'S NOT YOUR FRIEND AND SHE'S KISSING YOUR BROTHER.

TIP·PING POINT
(TIH-PING POYNT) NOUN

THE POINT WHEN AN OBJECT SHIFTS FROM ONE POSITION INTO A NEW, ENTIRELY DIFFERENT ONE.

AS IN: MY DAD SAYS THE **TIPPING POINT** OF OUR COUNTRY'S ECONOMY WAS HOUSING GAMBLERS AND GREEDY BANKERS.

AS IN: IF WE GET ONE **C** ON OUR REPORT CARDS, I'M AFRAID MOM WILL REACH HER **TIPPING POINT** AND THAT WILL BE THE END OF **BASKETBALL**.

AS IN: TODAY AT THE LIBRARY, I WENT UPSTAIRS, WALKED DOWN AN AISLE, PULLED **THE GIVER** OFF THE SHELF, AND FOUND MY **TIPPING POINT.**

THE MAIN REASON I CAN'T SLEEP

IS NOT BECAUSE OF THE **GAME** TOMORROW NIGHT, IS NOT BECAUSE THE STUBBLE ON MY HEAD FEELS LIKE **BUGS** ARE BREAK DANCING ON IT, IS NOT EVEN BECAUSE I'M **WORRIED** ABOUT DAD.

THE MAIN REASON I CAN'T SLEEP TONIGHT IS BECAUSE **JORDAN** IS ON THE PHONE WITH **MISS SWEET TEA** AND BETWEEN THE **GIGGLING** AND THE **BREATHING** HE TELLS HER HOW MUCH SHE'S THE APPLE OF HIS EYE AND THAT HE WANTS TO PEEL HER AND GET UNDER HER SKIN AND GIVE ME A BREAK...

I'M STILL HUNGRY AND RIGHT ABOUT NOW I WISH I HAD AN **APPLE** OF MY OWN.

SURPRISED

I HAVE IT ALL PLANNED OUT. WHEN WE WALK TO THE GAME I WILL TALK TO **JB** MAN TO MAN ABOUT HOW HE'S SPENDING WAY MORE TIME WITH **ALEXIS** THAN WITH ME AND **DAD**.

EXCEPT WHEN I HEAR THE **HORN**, I LOOK OUTSIDE MY WINDOW AND IT'S **RAINING**

AND **JB** IS JUMPING INTO A CAR WITH **MISS SWEET TEA** AND HER DAD, RUINING MY **PLAN**.

CONVERSATION

IN THE CAR I ASK DAD IF GOING TO THE DOCTOR WILL KILL HIM.

HE TELLS ME HE DOESN'T TRUST DOCTORS, THAT MY GRANDFATHER DID AND LOOK WHERE IT GOT HIM:

SIX FEET UNDER AT FORTY-FIVE.

BUT MOM SAYS YOUR DAD WAS REALLY SICK, I TELL HIM, AND DAD JUST ROLLS HIS EYES, SO I TRY SOMETHING DIFFERENT.

I TELL HIM THAT JUST BECAUSE YOUR TEAMMATE GETS FOULED ON A LAY-UP DOESN'T MEAN YOU SHOULDN'T EVER DRIVE TO THE LANE AGAIN.

HE LOOKS AT ME AND LAUGHS SO LOUD, WE ALMOST DON'T HEAR THE FLASHING BLUES BEHIND US.

GAME TIME: 6:00 P.M.

AT 5:28 P.M. A COP PULLS US OVER BECAUSE DAD HAS A BROKEN **TAILLIGHT**.

AT 5:30 THE OFFICER APPROACHES OUR CAR AND ASKS **DAD** FOR HIS **DRIVER'S LICENSE** AND **REGISTRATION**.

AT 5:32 THE TEAM LEAVES THE **LOCKER ROOM** AND PREGAME WARM-UPS BEGIN WITHOUT **ME**.

AT 5:34
DAD EXPLAINS TO THE
OFFICER THAT HIS LICENSE
IS IN HIS WALLET, WHICH IS
IN HIS JACKET AT HOME.

AT 5:37
DAD SAYS, LOOK, SIR,
MY NAME IS **CHUCK BELL**,
AND I'M JUST TRYING TO
GET MY BOY TO HIS
BASKETBALL GAME.

AT 5:47
WHILE COACH LEADS THE
WILDCATS IN TEAM PRAYER,
I PRAY DAD WON'T GET ARRESTED.

AT 5:48
THE COP SMILES AFTER VERIFYING
DAD'S IDENTITY ON GOOGLE,
AND SAYS, YOU "DA MAN"!

AT 5:50
DAD AUTOGRAPHS
A KRISPY KREME NAPKIN FOR
THE OFFICER AND GETS A
WARNING FOR HIS BROKEN
TAILLIGHT.
Chuck
AT 6:01
WE ARRIVE AT THE GAME BUT ON
MY SPRINT INTO THE GYM
I SLIP AND FALL IN
THE MUD.
SPLAT!

THIS IS MY SECOND YEAR

PLAYING FOR THE REGGIE LEWIS **WILDCATS** AND I'VE STARTED EVERY GAME UNTIL TONIGHT, WHEN COACH TELLS ME TO GO GET CLEANED UP THEN FIND A SEAT ON THE BENCH.

WHEN I TRY TO TELL HIM IT WASN'T MY **FAULT**, HE DOESN'T WANT TO HEAR ABOUT **SIRENS** AND BROKEN **TAILLIGHTS**.

JOSH, BETTER AN HOUR TOO SOON THAN A MINUTE TOO LATE, HE SAYS, TURNING HIS ATTENTION BACK TO **JB** AND THE GUYS ON THE COURT, ALL OF WHOM ARE POINTING AND LAUGHING AT ME.

BASKETBALL RULE #6

A GREAT TEAM HAS A GOOD SCORER WITH A TEAMMATE WHO'S ON POINT AND READY TO ASSIST.

JOSH'S PLAY-BY-PLAY

AT THE BEGINNING OF THE SECOND HALF WE'RE UP
TWENTY-THREE TO TWELVE.

I ENTER THE GAME FOR THE FIRST TIME.
I'M JUST HAPPY TO BE BACK ON THE FLOOR.

WHEN MY BROTHER AND I ARE ON THE
COURT TOGETHER THIS TEAM IS
UNSTOPPABLE, UNFADEABLE.

AND, YES, UNDEFEATED. **JB** BRINGS THE
BALL UP THE COURT. PASSES THE BALL TO **VONDIE**.

HE SHOOTS IT BACK TO **JB**. I CALL
FOR THE BALL. **JB** FINDS ME IN
THE **CORNER**.

I KNOW Y'ALL THINK IT'S TIME FOR THE
PICK-AND-ROLL, BUT I GOT SOMETHING
ELSE IN MIND. I GET THE BALL ON
THE **LEFT** SIDE.

JB IS SETTING THE **PICK**.

HERE IT COMES—

129

I ROLL TO HIS **RIGHT.**

THE **DOUBLE-TEAM** IS ON ME, LEAVING **JB** FREE.

HE'S GOT HIS HANDS IN THE AIR, LOOKING FOR THE **DISH** FROM ME.

DAD LIKES TO SAY, WHEN **JORDAN BELL** IS OPEN YOU CAN TAKE HIS THREE TO THE BANK, CASH IT IN, 'CAUSE IT'S ALL **MONEY.**

TONIGHT, I'M GOING FOR **BROKE.**

I SEE **JB**'S STILL WIDE OPEN.

McDONALD'S DRIVE-THRU OPEN.

BUT I GOT MY OWN PLANS.

THE **DOUBLE-TEAM** IS STILL ON ME LIKE **FEATHERS** ON A **BIRD.**

EVER SEEN AN **EAGLE SOAR**? SO **HIGH,** SO **FLY.** ME AND MY WINGS ARE— AND THAT'S WHEN I REMEMBER:

MY. WINGS. ARE. GONE.

COACH HAWKINS IS OUT OF HIS **SEAT.**

DAD IS ON HIS FEET, **SCREAMING. JB**'S **SCREAMING.**

THE CROWD'S **SCREAMING,** **FILTHY, PASS THE BALL!**

THE SHOT CLOCK IS AT **5**.
I DRIBBLE OUT OF THE
DOUBLE-TEAM.
4
EVERYTHING COMES TO A HEAD.
3
I SEE JORDAN.
2
YOU WANT IT THAT **BAD?**

HERE YA GO!

1...

BEFORE

TODAY, I WALK INTO THE GYM COVERED IN MORE DIRT THAN A CHIMNEY.

WHEN **JB** SCREAMS **FILTHY'S MCNASTY,** THE WHOLE **TEAM** LAUGHS.

EVEN **COACH.**

THEN I GET **BENCHED** FOR THE ENTIRE **FIRST HALF.** FOR BEING LATE.

TODAY, I WATCH AS WE TAKE A BIG LEAD, AND **JB** MAKES FOUR **THREES** IN A **ROW.**

I HEAR THE CROWD CHEER FOR **JB,** ESPECIALLY **DAD** AND **MOM.**

131

THEN I SEE JB WINK AT **MISS SWEET TEA** AFTER HE HITS A STUPID FREE THROW.

TODAY, I FINALLY GET INTO THE GAME AT THE START OF THE SECOND HALF.

JB SETS A WICKED PICK FOR ME JUST LIKE COACH SHOWED US IN PRACTICE, AND I GET DOUBLE-TEAMED ON THE ROLL JUST LIKE WE EXPECT.

TODAY, I WATCH JB GET OPEN AND WAVE FOR ME TO PASS.

INSTEAD I DRIBBLE, TRYING TO GET OUT OF THE **TRAP**, AND WATCH AS COACH AND DAD SCREAM FOR ME TO **PASS**.

TODAY, I PLAN ON PASSING THE BALL TO JB, BUT WHEN I HEAR HIM SAY

"FILTHY, GIVE ME THE BALL."

I DRIBBLE OVER TO MY BROTHER AND FIRE A PASS SO HARD,

IT LEVELS HIM, THE BLOOD FROM HIS NOSE STILL SHOOTING LONG AFTER THE SHOT-CLOCK BUZZER GOES OFF.

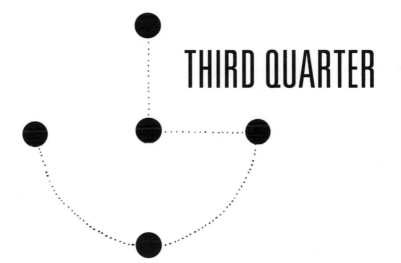

THIRD QUARTER

AFTER

ON THE SHORT RIDE HOME FROM THE HOSPITAL
THERE IS NO JAZZ MUSIC OR HOOP TALK, ONLY BRUTAL SILENCE,
THE UNSPOKEN WORDS VOLCANIC AND WEIGHTY.

DAD AND MOM, SOLEMN AND WOUNDED.

JB, BANDAGED AND HURT, LEANS AGAINST HIS BACK-SEAT WINDOW
AND WITH LESS THAN TWO FEET BETWEEN US I FEEL MILES AWAY FROM
ALL OF THEM.

SUSPENSION

SIT DOWN, MOM SAYS.
FEELS LIKE WE'RE IN HER OFFICE.

CAN I MAKE YOU A SANDWICH?
BUT WE'RE IN THE KITCHEN.

YOU WANT A TALL GLASS OF
ORANGE SODA?

MOM DOESN'T EVER LET
US DRINK SODA.

EAT UP, BECAUSE THIS
MAY BE YOUR LAST MEAL.

HERE IT COMES...

BOYS WITH NO SELF-CONTROL BECOME MEN BEHIND BARS.
. . .

HAVE YOU LOST YOUR MIND, SON?
NO.

DID YOUR FATHER AND I RAISE YOU TO BE **CHURLISH?**
NO.

SO, WHAT'S BEEN WRONG WITH YOU THESE PAST FEW WEEKS?
. . .

PUT THAT SANDWICH DOWN AND ANSWER ME.
I GUESS I'VE BEEN JUST—

YOU'VE BEEN JUST WHAT? **DERANGED?**
UH—

DON'T "UH" ME! TALK LIKE YOU HAVE SOME SENSE.
I DIDN'T MEAN TO HURT HIM.

YOU COULD HAVE **PERMANENTLY** INJURED YOUR **BROTHER.**
I KNOW. I'M SORRY, MOM.

YOU'RE SORRY FOR **WHAT?** I'M CONFUSED, JOSH.
MAKE ME UNDERSTAND. WHEN DID YOU BECOME A **THUG?**
I DON'T KNOW. I JUST WAS A LITTLE ANG—

ARE YOU GOING TO GET "ANGRY"
EVERY TIME JB HAS A GIRLFRIEND?
IT WASN'T JUST THAT.

THEN WHAT WAS IT?
I'M WAITING.
I DON'T KNOW.

OKAY, WELL, SINCE YOU DON'T
KNOW, HERE'S WHAT I KNOW —
I JUST GOT A LITTLE UPSET.

NOT GOOD ENOUGH. YOUR BEHAVIOR WAS UNACCEPTABLE.
I SAID I'M SORRY.

INDEED YOU DID. BUT YOU NEED TO TELL YOUR BROTHER,
NOT ME.
I WILL.

THERE ARE ALWAYS CONSEQUENCES, JOSH.
**HERE IT COMES: DISHES FOR A WEEK, NO PHONE, OR,
WORSE, NO SUNDAYS AT THE REC.**

JOSH, YOU AND **JB** ARE GROWING UP.
I KNOW.

YOU'RE **TWINS**, NOT THE SAME PERSON.
**BUT THAT DOESN'T MEAN HE HAS TO STOP
LOVING ME.**

YOUR BROTHER WILL ALWAYS LOVE YOU, **JOSH.**
I GUESS.

BOYS WITH NO DISCIPLINE END UP IN **PRISON.**
YEAH, I HEARD YOU THE FIRST TIME.

DON'T YOU GET SMART WITH ME
AND END UP IN MORE TROUBLE.
**WHY ARE YOU ALWAYS TRYING
TO SCARE ME?**

WE'RE DONE. YOUR DAD IS WAITING
FOR YOU.
**OKAY, BUT WHAT ARE THE
CONSEQUENCES?**

YOU'RE SUSPENDED.
FROM SCHOOL?

FROM THE **TEAM.**

CHUR·LISH
(CHUHR-LISH) ADJECTIVE

HAVING A BAD TEMPER, AND BEING DIFFICULT TO WORK WITH.

AS IN: I WANTED A PAIR OF STEPHON MARBURY'S SNEAKERS (STARBURYS), BUT DAD CALLED HIM A SELFISH MILLIONAIRE WITH A **BAD ATTITUDE**, AND WHY WOULD I WANT TO BE ASSOCIATED WITH SUCH A **CHURLISH** CHOKE ARTIST.

AS IN: I DON'T UNDERSTAND HOW I WENT FROM ANNOYED TO **GRUMPY** TO DOWNRIGHT **CHURLISH**.

AS IN: HOW DO YOU **APOLOGIZE** TO YOUR TWIN BROTHER FOR BEING **CHURLISH**—FOR ALMOST **BREAKING** HIS NOSE?

THIS WEEK, I

GET MY REPORT CARD.
MAKE THE HONOR ROLL.

WATCH THE TEAM WIN GAME **NINE**.

VOLUNTEER AT THE **LIBRARY**.

EAT LUNCH ALONE
FIVE TIMES.

AVOID
MISS SWEET TEA.

WALK HOME BY **MYSELF**.

CLEAN THE GARAGE
DURING PRACTICE.

TRY TO **ATONE** DAY AND **NIGHT**.

SIT BESIDE **JB** AT DINNER.
HE **MOVES**.

TELL HIM A JOKE.
HE DOESN'T EVEN **SMILE**.

DO HIS **CHORES**.
HE PAYS NO
ATTENTION.

SAY I'M SORRY
BUT HE WON'T
LISTEN.

BASKETBALL RULE #7

REBOUNDING IS THE ART OF ANTICIPATING, OF ALWAYS BEING PREPARED TO GRAB IT. BUT YOU CAN'T DROP THE BALL.

THE NOSEBLEED SECTION

OUR SEATS ARE IN THE CLOUDS, AND EVERY TIME DAD THINKS THE REF MAKES A BAD CALL, HE RAINS.

ALL MOM DOES IS POP UP LIKE AN UMBRELLA, THEN DAD SITS BACK DOWN.

JB'S GOT NINETEEN POINTS, SIX REBOUNDS, AND THREE ASSISTS. HE'S ON FIRE, BLAZING FROM BASELINE TO BASELINE.

DAD SCREAMS, SOMEBODY NEEDS TO CALL THE FIRE DEPARTMENT, 'CAUSE JB IS BURNING UP THIS PLACE.

THE OTHER TEAM CALLS A TIME-OUT.

DAD, JB STILL WON'T SPEAK TO ME, I SAY.

RIGHT NOW JB CAN'T SEE YOU, SON, DAD SAYS.

YOU JUST HAVE TO LET THE SMOKE CLEAR, AND THEN HE'LL BE OKAY.

FOR NOW, WHY DON'T YOU WRITE HIM A LETTER?

GOOD IDEA, I THINK. BUT WHAT SHOULD I SAY? I ASK HIM.

BY THEN, DAD IS ON HIS FEET WITH THE REST OF THE GYM AS JB STEALS THE BALL AND TAKES OFF LIKE A WILDFIRE.

143

FAST BREAK

HE'S A
BACKCOURT BALLER
ON THE **BREAK**,
A **RUNNING**
GUNNING
SHOOTING STAR
FLYING FAST.

JB'S FIXING FOR THE **GLASS**—
BOUNCE BOUNCE BALL
BESIDE HIM, **NOW** HE'S
GETTING FLYER AND
FLYER, CLIMBING SKY.

HE NODS HIS HEAD AND **PUMPS**
A **FAKE**, EXPLODES THE LANE.

CRISS BALL CROSS BALL CRISS
AND TAKES THE **BREAK**,

KABOOM

ABOVE THE **RIM**,
A **THUNDEROUS** ALMOST **DUNK**.
THAT ELBOW JUST SENT **JB**

KERPLUNK

TO THE FLOOR. FOUL.

STORM

LIKE A STRONG WIND, DAD RISES FROM THE CLOUDS, STRIKES DOWN THE STAIRS, SWIFT AND SHARP AND MAD AS LIGHTNING.

FLAGRANT FOUL, REF!

HE YELLS TO EVERYONE IN THE GYM.

NOW HE'S **HAIL** AND **BLIZZARD**. HIS FACE, **COLD** AND **HARD** AS **ICE**.

HIS HANDS **PULSING** THROUGH THE **AIR**.

HIS MOUTH, LOUD AS **THUNDER**.

HE **TACKLED** JB— THIS AIN'T FOOTBALL,

DAD ROARS IN THE **FACE** OF THE REF, WHILE **JB** AND HIS ATTACKER DO THE EYE DANCE.

I WANT TO JOIN IN, OFFER MY **SQUALL**, BUT MOM SHOOTS ME A LOOK THAT SAYS, **STAY OUT OF THE RAIN, SON.**

SO, I JUST **WATCH AS** SHE AND **COACH** CHASE DAD'S **TORNADO**.

I WATCH AS SHE WRAPS HER ARMS AROUND DAD'S **WAIST**.

I WATCH AS SHE SLOWLY BRINGS HIM BACK TO WIND AND CLOUD.

I WATCH MOM TAKE A TISSUE FROM HER PURSE TO WIPE HER TEARS, AND THE SUDDEN ONSET OF BLOOD FROM DAD'S NOSE.

THE NEXT MORNING

AT BREAKFAST MOM TELLS DAD, CALL DR. YOUNGBLOOD TODAY OR ELSE.

THE NAME'S IRONIC, I THINK. I'M SORRY FOR LOSING MY COOL, DAD TELLS US. JB ASKS MOM CAN HE GO TO THE MALL AFTER PRACTICE TODAY?

THERE'S A NEW VIDEO GAME WE CAN CHECK OUT, I SAY TO JB. HE HASN'T SPOKEN TO ME IN FIVE DAYS.

YOUR BROTHER HAS APOLOGIZED PROFUSELY FOR HIS MISTAKE, MOM SAYS TO JB.

TELL HIM THAT I SAW THE LOOK IN HIS EYES, AND IT WASN'T A MISTAKE, JB REPLIES.

PRO·FUSE·LY
(PRUH-FYOOS-LEE) ADVERB

POURING FORTH IN GREAT QUANTITY.

AS IN: **JB** GETS ALL NERVOUS AND SWEATS PROFUSELY EVERY TIME **MISS SWEET TEA** WALKS INTO A ROOM.

AS IN: THE TEAM HAS THANKED **JB** PROFUSELY FOR LEADING US INTO THE **PLAYOFFS.**

AS IN: MOM SAID DAD'S **BLOOD PRESSURE** WAS SO HIGH DURING THE GAME THAT WHEN HE WENT INTO A **RAGE** IT CAUSED HIS **NOSE** TO START **BLEEDING** **PROFUSELY.**

DAILY NEWS
DECEMBER 14

THE REGGIE LEWIS WILDCATS CAPPED OFF THEIR REMARKABLE SEASON WITH A FIERY WIN AGAINST OLIVE BRANCH JUNIOR HIGH.

PLAYING WITHOUT SUSPENDED PHENOM JOSH BELL DIDN'T SEEM TO FAZE COACH HAWKINS'S UNDEFEATED 'CATS.

AFTER A BRIEF MELEE CAUSED BY A HARD FOUL, JOSH'S TWIN, JORDAN, LED THE TEAM, LIKE

GW CROSSING THE DELAWARE, TO VICTORY, AND TO THEIR SECOND STRAIGHT PLAYOFF APPEARANCE.

WITH A FIRST-ROUND BYE, THEY BEGIN THEIR QUEST FOR THE COUNTY TROPHY NEXT WEEK AGAINST THE INDEPENDENCE RED ROCKETS, THE DEFENDING CHAMPIONS, WHILE PLAYING WITHOUT JOSH "FILTHY McNASTY" BELL, THE DAILY NEWS'S MOST VALUABLE PLAYER.

MOSTLY EVERYONE

IN CLASS APPLAUDS, CONGRATULATING ME ON BEING SELECTED AS THE **JUNIOR HIGH MVP** BY THE DAILY NEWS.

EVERYONE EXCEPT **MISS SWEET TEA**:

YOU'RE MEAN, JOSH!

AND I DON'T KNOW WHY THEY GAVE YOU THAT AWARD AFTER WHAT YOU DID TO **JORDAN.**

JERK!

JB LOOKS AT ME.

I WAIT FOR HIM TO SAY SOMETHING, ANYTHING IN DEFENSE OF HIS ONLY BROTHER.

BUT HIS EYES, EMPTY AS FIRED CANNONS, SHOOT WAY PAST ME.

SOMETIMES IT'S THE THINGS THAT AREN'T SAID THAT **KILL** YOU.

FINAL JEOPARDY

THE ONLY SOUNDS, TEETH
MUNCHING MELON AND
STRAWBERRY FROM MOM'S
FRUIT COCKTAIL DESSERT

AND ALEX TREBEK'S ANNOYING VOICE:
THIS FOURTEEN-TIME **NBA** ALL-STAR ALSO
PLAYED MINOR-LEAGUE BASEBALL FOR
THE **BIRMINGHAM BARONS.**

EVEN MOM KNOWS THE ANSWER.

HEY, DAD, THE PLAYOFFS START IN **TWO**
DAYS AND THE TEAM NEEDS ME, I SAY.

PLUS MY GRADES WERE GOOD.

JB ROLLS HIS EYES AND SAYS TO
ALEX WHAT WE ALL KNOW: WHO IS
"MICHAEL JEFFREY JORDAN"?

JOSH, THIS ISN'T ABOUT
YOUR **GRADES,** MOM SAYS.

HOW YOU **BEHAVE**
GOING FORWARD IS
WHAT MATTERS TO US.

I LOOOOVE CHRISTMAS.

CAN'T WAIT FOR YOUR MOTHER'S **MAPLE TURKEY**, DAD SAYS, TRYING TO BREAK THE **TENSION**.

NOBODY RESPONDS, SO HE CONTINUES: Y'ALL KNOW WHAT THE MAMA **TURKEY** SAID TO HER **NAUGHTY SON**?

IF YOUR PAPA COULD SEE YOU NOW, HE'D TURN OVER IN HIS **GRAVY**! NONE OF US LAUGH. THEN ALL OF US **LAUGH**.

CHUCK, YOU ARE A SILLY MAN, MOM SAYS.

JORDAN, WE WANT TO MEET YOUR NEW FRIEND, SHE ADDS.

YEAH, INVITE HER TO DINNER, DAD AGREES. **FILTHY** AND I WANT TO GET TO KNOW THE GIRL WHO STOLE **JB**.

STOP THAT, **CHUCK!** MOM SAYS, HITTING DAD ON THE **ARM**.

WHAT IS "I'LL THINK ABOUT IT"? **JB** REPLIES, KISSING MOM, **DAPPING** DAD, AND **NOT** ONCE LOOKING AT **ME**.

DEAR JORDAN

WITHOUT U
I AM EMPTY,
THE GOAL
WITH NO NET.
SEEMS
MY LIFE WAS
BROKEN,
SHATTERED,
LIKE PUZZLE PIECES
ON THE COURT.
I CAN NO LONGER FIT.
CAN YOU
HELP ME HEAL,
RUN WITH ME,
SLASH WITH ME
LIKE WE USED TO?
LIKE TWO STARS
STEALING SUN,
LIKE TWO BROTHERS
BURNING UP.
TOGETHER.
P.S. I'M SORRY.

153

I DON'T KNOW

IF HE READ MY LETTER, BUT THIS MORNING ON THE BUS TO SCHOOL WHEN I SAID, **VONDIE**, YOUR HEAD IS SO **BIG**, YOU DON'T HAVE A FOREHEAD, YOU HAVE A **FIVE-HEAD**, I COULD FEEL **JB** LAUGHING A LITTLE.

NO PIZZA AND FRIES

THE **SPINACH** AND **TOFU** SALAD MOM PACKED FOR MY LUNCH TODAY IS **CRUEL**, BUT NOT AS **CRUEL** AS THE **EVIL** LOOK **MISS SWEET TEA** SHOOTS ME FROM ACROSS THE **CAFETERIA**.

EVEN VONDIE

HAS A GIRLFRIEND NOW.
SHE WANTS TO BE A DOCTOR ONE DAY.

SHE'S A CANDY STRIPER AND A
CHEERLEADER AND A TALKER

WITH SKINNY LEGS AND A MOUTH AS
BIG AS VERMONT,

WHICH ACCORDING TO HER HAS THE
BEST TOMATOES,

WHICH SHE CLAIMS COME IN ALL
COLORS, EVEN PURPLE,

WHICH SHE TELLS ME IS HER FAVORITE
COLOR,

WHICH I ALREADY KNOW BECAUSE OF
HER HAIR.

THIS IS STILL BETTER THAN HAVING
NO GIRLFRIEND AT ALL.

WHICH IS WHAT I HAVE NOW.

UH-OH

WHILE I'M ON THE PHONE WITH **VONDIE** TALKING ABOUT MY CHANCES OF PLAYING IN ANOTHER GAME THIS SEASON, I HEAR PANTING COMING FROM MOM AND DAD'S ROOM, BUT WE DON'T OWN A **DOG**.

I RUN INTO DAD'S ROOM

TO SEE WHAT ALL THE **NOISE** IS AND FIND HIM **KNEELING** ON THE **FLOOR**, RUBBING A TOWEL IN THE **RUG**.

IT **REEKS** OF **VOMIT**.

YOU THREW UP, **DAD**? I ASK.

MUST HAVE BEEN SOMETHING I ATE.

HE SITS UP ON THE BED, HOLDS HIS CHEST LIKE HE'S **PLEDGING** ALLEGIANCE. ONLY THERE'S **NO FLAG**.

Y'ALL READY TO **EAT**? HE MUTTERS.

YOU OKAY, DAD? I ASK.

HE NODS AND SHOWS ME A LETTER HE'S READING.

DAD, WAS THAT YOU **COUGHING**?

I'VE GOT GREAT NEWS, FILTHY.

WHAT IS IT? I ASK.

I GOT A COACHING OFFER AT A NEARBY COLLEGE STARTING NEXT MONTH.

A JOB? WHAT ABOUT THE HOUSE? WHAT ABOUT MOM? WHAT ABOUT ME AND JB?
WHO'S GONNA SHOOT FREE THROWS WITH US EVERY NIGHT? I ASK.

FILTHY, YOU AND JB ARE GETTING OLDER, MORE MATURE—YOU'LL MANAGE, HE SAYS. AND, WHAT'S WITH THE SWITCH? FIRST YOU WANT ME TO GET A JOB, NOW YOU DON'T? WHAT'S UP, FILTHY?

DAD, MOM THINKS YOU SHOULD TAKE IT EASY, FOR YOUR HEALTH, RIGHT?

I MEAN, DIDN'T YOU MAKE A MILLION DOLLARS PLAYING BASKETBALL? YOU DON'T REALLY NEED TO WORK.

FILTHY, WHAT I NEED IS TO GET BACK ON THE COURT. THAT'S WHAT YOUR DAD NEEDS!

I PREFER TO BE CALLED JOSH, DAD. NOT FILTHY.

OH, REALLY, FILTHY? HE LAUGHS. I'M SERIOUS, DAD—PLEASE DON'T CALL ME THAT NAME ANYMORE.

YOU GONNA TAKE THE JOB, DAD?

SON, I MISS "SWISH."
I MISS THE SMELL OF
ORANGE LEATHER.

I MISS EATIN' UP CATS WHO
THINK THEY CAN RUN WITH
DA MAN.

THE COURT IS MY KITCHEN. SON, I
MISS BEING THE TOP CHEF.

SO, YEAH, I'M GONNA TAKE IT...
IF YOUR MOTHER LET'S ME.

WELL, I WILL TALK TO HER ABOUT
THIS JOB THING, SINCE IT MEANS
SO MUCH TO YOU.

BUT, YOU KNOW SHE'S REALLY WORRIED ABOUT YOU, DAD.

FILTH—I MEAN JOSH, OKAY, YOU TALK TO HER, HE LAUGHS.

AND MAYBE, IN RETURN, DAD, YOU CAN TALK TO HER ABOUT
LETTING ME BACK ON THE TEAM FOR THE PLAYOFFS.

I FEEL LIKE I'M LETTING MY TEAMMATES DOWN.

YOU LET YOUR FAMILY DOWN TOO, JOSH,
HE REPLIES, STILL HOLDING HIS CHEST.

SO WHAT SHOULD I DO, DAD?
I ASK.

WELL, RIGHT NOW YOU SHOULD GO
SET THE DINNER TABLE, MOM
SAYS, STANDING AT THE DOOR
WATCHING DAD WITH EYES
FULL OF PANIC.

BEHIND CLOSED DOORS

WE DECIDED NO MORE BASKETBALL, CHUCK, MOM YELLS.
BABY, IT'S NOT BALL, IT'S COACHING, DAD TELLS HER.

IT'S STILL STRESS. YOU DON'T NEED TO BE ON THE COURT.
THE DOCTOR SAID IT'S FINE, BABY.

WHAT DOCTOR? WHEN DID YOU GO TO THE DOCTOR?
I GO A COUPLE TIMES A WEEK. DR. WEBMD.

ARE YOU SERIOUS! THIS IS NOT SOME JOKE, CHARLES.
. . .

GOING ONLINE IS NOT GOING TO SAVE YOUR LIFE.
TRUTH IS, I'VE HAD ENOUGH OF THIS TALK ABOUT ME
BEING SICK.

SO HAVE I. I'M SCHEDULING AN APPOINTMENT FOR YOU.

FINE!

I SHOULDN'T BE SO WORRIED ABOUT YOUR
HEART— IT'S YOUR HEAD THAT'S CRAZY.

CRAZY FOR YOU, LIL' MAMA.

STOP THAT. I SAID STOP. IT'S TIME
FOR DINNER, CHUCK . . . OOOH.

WHO'S DA MAN?

AND THEN THERE IS SILENCE, SO I GO
SET THE DINNER TABLE, BECAUSE
WHEN THEY STOP TALKING,
I KNOW WHAT THAT MEANS.
UGGGHH!

THE GIRL WHO STOLE MY BROTHER

IS HER NEW NAME. SHE'S NO LONGER SWEET. BITTER IS HER TASTE.

EVEN WORSE, SHE ASKS FOR SECONDS OF VEGETABLE LASAGNA,
WHICH MAKES MOM SMILE 'CAUSE **JB** AND I CAN'T GET WITH THIS
WHOLE BETTER-EATING THING AND WE NEVER ASK FOR SECONDS
UNTIL TONIGHT, WHEN **JB**, STILL GRINNING AND **CHEESING** FOR SOME
INVISIBLE CAMERA THAT **MISS BITTER(SWEET) TEA** HOLDS, ASKS FOR
MORE SALAD, WHICH MAKES DAD LAUGH AND PROMPTS MOM
TO ASK, HOW DID YOU TWO **MEET**?

SURPRISINGLY, **JB** IS A MOTOR MOUTH, GIVING US ALL THE DETAILS
ABOUT THAT FIRST TIME IN THE CAFETERIA:

SHE CAME INTO THE LUNCHROOM.

IT WAS HER FIRST DAY AT OUR SCHOOL, AND WE JUST STARTED TALKING
ABOUT ALL KINDS OF STUFF, AND SHE SAID SHE PLAYED BASKETBALL
AT HER LAST SCHOOL, AND THEN **VONDIE** WAS LIKE, "**JB**, SHE'S **HOT**,"
AND I WAS LIKE, "YEAH, SHE IS KINDA **PULCHRITUDINOUS**."

AND FOR THE FIRST TIME IN FIFTEEN DAYS, **JB** LOOKS AT ME FOR A
SPLIT SECOND, AND I ALMOST SEE THE HINT OF A SMILE.

THINGS I LEARN AT DINNER

SHE WENT TO NIKE HOOPS CAMP FOR GIRLS. HER FAVORITE PLAYER IS SKYLAR DIGGINS.

SHE CAN NAME EACH OF THE 2010 NBA CHAMPION LAKERS.

HER DAD WENT TO COLLEGE WITH SHAQUILLE O'NEAL. SHE KNOWS HOW TO DO A CROSSOVER.

HER AAU TEAM WON A CHAMPIONSHIP. SHE'S GOT GAME. HER PARENTS ARE DIVORCED.

SHE'S GOING TO VISIT HER MOM NEXT WEEK FOR CHRISTMAS BREAK. SHE LIVES WITH HER DAD.

SHE SHOOTS HOOPS AT THE REC TO RELAX.

HER MOM DOESN'T WANT HER PLAYING BASKETBALL.

HER DAD'S COMING TO OUR GAME TOMORROW TO SEE JB PLAY.

SHE'S SORRY I WON'T BE PLAYING.

HER SMILE IS AS SWEET AS MOM'S CARROT CAKE.

SHE SMELLS LIKE SUGARPLUM.

SHE HAS A SISTER IN COLLEGE.

HER SISTER GOES TO DUKE.

DISHES

WHEN THE LAST PLATE IS SCRUBBED, THE LEFTOVERS PUT UP, AND THE FLOOR SWEPT CLEAN, MOM COMES INTO THE **KITCHEN**.

WHEN IS DAD'S DOCTOR APPOINTMENT? I ASK.

JOSH, YOU KNOW I DON'T LIKE YOU **EAVESDROPPING**.

I GET IT FROM YOU, MOM, I SAY.

AND SHE LAUGHS, 'CAUSE SHE KNOWS I'M NOT SAYING NOTHING BUT THE **TRUTH**. IT'S **NEXT WEEK**.

SCHOOL'S OUT NEXT WEEK. MAYBE I CAN GO WITH YOU TO THE DOCTOR?
MAYBE, SHE SAYS.

I PUT THE BROOM DOWN, WRAP MY ARMS AROUND HER, AND TELL HER **THANK YOU**.

FOR LOVING US, AND DAD, AND LETTING US PLAY BASKETBALL, AND BEING THE BEST MOTHER IN THE **WORLD**.

KEEP THIS UP, SHE SAYS, AND YOU'LL BE BACK ON THE COURT IN NO TIME.

DOES THAT MEAN I CAN PLAY IN TOMORROW'S **PLAYOFF GAME?** I ASK.

DON'T PRESS YOUR LUCK, SON. IT'S GOING TO TAKE MORE THAN A **HUG**. NOW HELP ME DRY THESE **DISHES**.

COACH'S TALK BEFORE THE GAME

TONIGHT I DECIDE TO SIT ON THE BENCH WITH THE TEAM DURING THE GAME INSTEAD OF THE BLEACHERS WITH DAD AND MOM, WHO'S SITTING NEXT TO HIM JUST IN CASE HE DECIDES TO ACT **CHURLISH AGAIN.**

COACH SAYS:
WE'VE WON TEN GAMES IN A ROW.
THE DIFFERENCE BETWEEN A WINNING STREAK AND A LOSING STREAK IS ONE GAME.

NOW, JOSH IS NOT WITH US AGAIN, SO SOMEBODY'S GONNA HAVE TO STEP UP IN THE LOW POST.

I SIT BACK DOWN ON THE BENCH
AND WATCH **JB** LEAD OUR **WILDCATS** TO
THE **COURT**.

WHEN THE GAME FINALLY STARTS, I GLANCE UP
AT DAD AND MOM, BUT THEY'RE NOT THERE.

WHEN I LOOK BACK AT THE COURT,
JB IS STARING AT ME
LIKE WE'VE BOTH JUST SEEN
ANOTHER GHOST.

JOSH'S PLAY-BY-PLAY

THE TEAM'S IN TROUBLE. IF THEY DON'T
FIND AN ANSWER SOON OUR CHAMPIONSHIP
DREAMS ARE OVER.

DOWN BY **THREE**, THEY'RE PLAYING LIKE
KITTENS, NOT **WILDCATS**.

WITH LESS THAN A MINUTE TO GO VONDIE
BRINGS THE BALL UP THE COURT. WILL HE
GO INSIDE FOR A QUICK **TWO** OR GET THE
BALL TO **JB** FOR THE THREE-BALL?

HE PASSES THE BALL TO NUMBER TWENTY-NINE
ON THE RIGHT WING AND TRIES TO **DRIBBLE OUT**,
BUT THE DEFENSE IS SUFFOCATING.

THEY'RE ON HIM LIKE
BLACK ON **MIDNIGHT**.

HE SHOOTS IT OVER TO **JB**, WHO
LOOKS UP AT THE CLOCK. HE'S GONNA
LET IT GET AS CLOSE AS POSSIBLE.

THEY'VE GOTTA MISS ME RIGHT NOW.

VONDIE COMES OVER, SETS A HIGH
PICK. JB'S OPEN, HE'S GONNA TAKE
THE **THREE**. IT'S UP.

THAT'S A GOOD-LOOKING BALL THERE.

BUT NOT GOOD ENOUGH.
IT CLANGS OFF THE RIM.
THE BUZZER RINGS AND THE
WILDCATS LOSE THE FIRST HALF.

TEXT MESSAGES FROM MOM, PART ONE

7:04
DAD WASN'T FEELING WELL,
SO WE WENT OUTSIDE FOR SOME AIR. BACK SOON.

7:17
I THINK WE'RE HEADING HOME.
AT HALFTIME, LET YOUR BROTHER KNOW.

7:45
HOME NOW. DAD WANTS TO KNOW THE SCORE.
HOW IS JORDAN DOING? YOU OKAY?

7:47
Y'ALL HANG IN THERE. THE SECOND HALF WILL BE BETTER.
HI TO ALEXIS. GET

7:47
A RIDE WITH COACH
OR VONDIE. YES, DAD'S OKAY. I THINK.
SEE YOU SOON.

7:48
I SHOULDN'T HAVE SAID
"I THINK." HE'S FINE, JUST TIRED.
HE SAYS DON'T COME HOME

7:48
IF YOU LOSE. LOL.

166

THE SECOND HALF

VONDIE STRIPS THE BALL AT CENTER COURT, SHOOTS A SHORT PASS TO **JB**, WHO SKIPS

DOWNTOWN
ZIPS
AROUND,

THEN DOUBLE DIPS IT IN THE BOWL.

SWOOSH

MAN, THAT WAS COLD.
WE'RE UP BY **TWO**.
THESE CATS ARE **BALLING**.

JB IS ON **FIRE**, TAKING THE SCORE HIGHER AND **HIGHER**, AND THE TEAM AND COACH AND **ALEXIS** AND **ME**...
WE'RE HIS **CHOIR**.

WILDCATS! WILDCATS!

MY BROTHER IS SUPERMAN TONIGHT, **SLIDING** AND **GLIDING** INTO RARE AIR, LIGHTING UP THE SKY AND THE SCOREBOARD.

SAVING THE WORLD AND OUR CHANCE AT A CHAMPIONSHIP.

TOMORROW IS THE LAST DAY OF SCHOOL BEFORE CHRISTMAS VACATION

TONIGHT, I'M STUDYING. USUALLY I HELP JB PREPARE FOR HIS TESTS, BUT SINCE THE INCIDENT HE'S BEEN STUDYING ALONE, WHICH HAS ME A LITTLE SCARED BECAUSE TOMORROW IS ALSO THE BIG VOCABULARY STANDARDS **TEST**.

(BUT DON'T SAY THAT WORD AROUND MOM.

SHE THINKS THAT "STANDARDS" ARE A LOUSY IDEA.)

SO, AFTER THE GAME I GO HOME AND PULL OUT MY STUDY SHEET WITH ALL THE WORDS WE'VE BEEN STUDYING AND MY CLUES TO REMEMBER THEM. LIKE **HEIRLOOM**.

AS IN: DAD TREATS HIS CHAMPIONSHIP RING LIKE SOME KIND OF FAMILY **HEIRLOOM** THAT WE CAN'T WEAR UNTIL ONE OF US BECOMES **DA MAN**.

I PUT EIGHT PAGES OF WORDS ON JB'S PILLOW WHILE HE'S BRUSHING HIS TEETH, THEN TURN OFF MY **LIGHT** AND GO TO **SLEEP**.

WHEN HE CLIMBS INTO BED, I HEAR THE SOUND OF **RUFFLING** PAPER.

THEN HIS NIGHT-LIGHT COMES ON AND I DON'T HEAR ANYTHING ELSE EXCEPT **THANKS**.

COACH COMES OVER

TO MY TABLE DURING LUNCH, SITS DOWN WITH A BAG FROM
McDONALD'S, HANDS ME A FRY AND VONDIE A FRY, BITES INTO
HIS **McRIB** SANDWICH, AND SAYS:

LOOK, JOSH, YOU AND YOUR BROTHER NEED TO SQUASH THIS **BEEF.**
IF MY TWO STARS AREN'T ALIGNED, THERE'S NO WAY
THE UNIVERSE IS KIND TO US.

HUH? VONDIE SAYS.

MY BROTHER AND I GOT INTO A **BAD**
FIGHT WHEN WE WERE IN HIGH SCHOOL,
AND WE'VE BEEN **ESTRANGED**
EVER SINCE.
YOU WANT THAT?

I SHAKE MY HEAD.

THEN FIX IT, **FILTHY**. FIX IT **FAST**. WE DON'T NEED ANY DISTRACTIONS ON THIS JOURNEY. AND WHILE YOU'RE WORKING ON THAT, GIVE YOUR MOM SOMETHING SPECIAL THIS **HOLIDAY**.

SHE SAYS YOU'VE SERVED YOUR SENTENCE WELL AND THAT SHE'LL CONSIDER LETTING YOU BACK ON THE TEAM IF WE MAKE IT TO THE **CHAMPIONSHIP GAME**.

MERRY CHRISTMAS, **JOSH**.

ES·TRANGED

[IH-STREYNJD] ADJECTIVE

THE INTERRUPTION OF A BOND, WHEN ONE PERSON BECOMES A STRANGER TO SOMEONE WHO WAS CLOSE: A RELATIVE, FRIEND, OR LOVED ONE.

AS IN: ALEXIS'S MOM AND DAD ARE **ESTRANGED**.

AS IN: WHEN I THREW THE BALL AT **JB**, I THINK I WAS **ESTRANGED** FROM MYSELF, IF THAT'S **POSSIBLE**.

AS IN: EVEN THOUGH **JB** AND I ARE **ESTRANGED,** DAD'S MAKING US **PLAY** TOGETHER IN A THREE-ON-THREE TOURNAMENT ON THE **REC** PLAYGROUND **TOMORROW.**

SCHOOL'S OUT

MOM HAS TO WORK LATE, SO DAD PICKS US UP.
EVEN THOUGH **JB**'S STILL NOT TALKING TO ME, DAD'S CRACKING JOKES
AND WE'RE BOTH LAUGHING LIKE IT'S THE GOOD OL' TIMES.

WHAT ARE WE GETTING FOR CHRISTMAS, DAD? **JB** ASKS.
WHAT WE ALWAYS GET. BOOKS, I REPLY,
AND WE BOTH LAUGH JUST LIKE THE GOOD OL' TIMES.

BOYS, YOUR TALENT WILL HELP YOU WIN GAMES, DAD SAYS, BUT YOUR INTELLIGENCE, THAT WILL HELP YOU WIN AT **LIFE**.

WHO SAID THAT? I ASK.

I SAID IT, DIDN'T YOU HEAR ME?

MICHAEL JORDAN SAID IT, **JB** SAYS, STILL LOOKING AT DAD.

LOOK, BOYS, YOU'VE BOTH DONE GOOD IN SCHOOL THIS **YEAR**, AND YOUR MOM AND I APPRECIATE THAT.

SO YOU CHOOSE A GIFT, AND I'LL GET IT.

YOU MEAN NO BOOKS? I ASK. **YES!**

NOPE. YOU'RE STILL GETTING THE **BOOKS**, PLAYER. SANTA'S JUST LETTING YOU PICK SOMETHING EXTRA.

AT THE STOPLIGHT, **JB** AND I LOOK OUT THE WINDOW AT THE EXACT MOMENT WE PASS BY THE MALL AND I KNOW EXACTLY WHAT **JB** WANTS.

DAD, CAN WE STOP AT THAT SNEAKER STORE IN THE MALL?

YEAH, DAD, CAN **WE?** **JB** ECHOES.

AND THE WORD **WE** NEVER SOUNDED **SWEETER.**

THE PHONE RINGS

MOM'S DECORATING THE **TREE,**

DAD'S OUTSIDE SHOOTING FREE THROWS,
WARMING UP FOR THE **TOURNAMENT.**

HELLO, I ANSWER.
HI, **JOSH,** SHE REPLIES. MAY I PLEASE
SPEAK WITH **PRECIOUS?**

HE'S, UH, BUSY RIGHT NOW, I TELL HER.

WELL, JUST TELL HIM I WILL SEE HIM AT
THE **REC,** SHE SAYS, AND NOW I
UNDERSTAND WHY JB'S TAKING HIS
SECOND SHOWER THIS MORNING
WHEN HE **BARELY** TAKES **ONE**
MOST SCHOOL MORNINGS.

BASKETBALL RULE #8

SOMETIMES YOU HAVE TO LEAN BACK A LITTLE AND FADE AWAY TO GET THE BEST SHOT.

WHEN WE GET TO THE COURT

I CHALLENGE DAD TO A QUICK GAME OF ONE-ON-ONE BEFORE THE TOURNAMENT SO WE CAN BOTH WARM UP.

HE LAUGHS AND SAYS, CHECK, THEN GIVES ME THE BALL, BUT IT HITS ME IN THE CHEST BECAUSE I'M BUSY LOOKING OVER AT THE SWINGS WHERE JORDAN AND MISS SWEET TEA ARE TALKING AND HOLDING HANDS.

PAY ATTENTION, FILTHY— I MEAN JOSH.

I'M ABOUT TO CLEAN YOU UP, BOY, DAD SAYS.

I PUMP FAKE HIM THEN SUGAR SHAKE HIM FOR AN EASY TWO.

I HEAR APPLAUSE.

KIDS ARE COMING OVER TO WATCH.

ON THE NEXT PLAY I SWITCH IT UP AND LAUNCH A THREE FROM DOWNTOWN.

IT ROLLS ROUND AND ROUND AND IN.

THE BENCHES ARE FILLING UP.

EVEN JORDAN AND ALEXIS ARE NOW WATCHING.

FIVE-OH IS THE SCORE, THIRD PLAY OF THE GAME.

I TRY MY CROSSOVER, BUT

DAD STEALS THE BALL LIKE A THIEF IN THE NIGHT, CAMPS OUT AT THE TOP FOR A MINUTE.

WHAT YOU DOING, OLD MAN? I SAY.

DON'T WORRY 'BOUT ME, SON. I'M CONTEMPLATIN', PREPARING TO SHUT DOWN ALL YOUR PLAYA HATIN', DAD SAYS.

SON, I EVER TELL YOU ABOUT THIS CAT NAMED WILLIE I PLAYED WITH IN ITALY?

AND BEFORE I CAN ANSWER HE UNLEASHES A KILLER CROSSOVER, LEAVING ME WISHING FOR A CUSHION.

THE KIDS ARE OFF THE BENCHES.

ON THEIR FEET HOLLERIN',

OHHHHHHH, WHOOP WHOOP!

MEET THE PRESS, JOSH BELL, DAD LAUGHS, ON HIS WAY TO THE HOOP.

BUT THEN—

AT NOON, IN THE GYM, WITH DAD

PEOPLE WATCHING
PLAYERS BOASTING
ME SCORING
DAD SNORING
CROWD GROWING
WE BALLING
ME PUMPING
DAD JUMPING
ME FAKING
NASTY SHOT
NASTY MOVES
FIVE-ZERO
MY LEAD
NEXT PLAY
DRIBBLE BOUNCE
DRIBBLE STEAL
DAD LAUGHS
PALMS BALL
YOU OKAY?
DAD WINKS
WATCH THIS
HE DIPS
SWEAT DRIPS
LEFT Y'ALL
RIGHT Y'ALL

I FALL
CROWD WILD
DAD DRIVES
STEPS STRIDES
RUNS FAST
HOOP BOUND
STUTTER STEPS
LETS LOOSE
SCREAMS LOUD
STANDS STILL

BREATH SHORT
MORE SWEAT
GRABS CHEST
EYES ROLL
BALL DROPS
DAD DROPS
I SCREAM
"HELP, PLEASE"

SWEET TEA
DIALS CELL
JORDAN RUNS
BRINGS WATER
SPLASHES FACE
DAD NOTHING
OUT COLD
I REMEMBER
GYM CLASS
TILT PINCH
BLOW PUMP
BLOW PUMP
STILL NOTHING
BLOW PUMP
SIRENS BLAST
PULSE GONE
EYES SHUT.

FOURTH QUARTER

THE DOCTOR PATS JORDAN AND ME ON THE BACK AND SAYS

YOUR DAD SHOULD BE FINE. IF YOU'RE LUCKY, YOU BOYS WILL BE FISHING WITH HIM IN NO TIME.

WE DON'T FISH, I TELL HIM. MOM SHOOTS ME A MEAN LOOK.

MRS. BELL, THE MYOCARDIAL INFARCTION HAS CAUSED SOME COMPLICATIONS. YOUR HUSBAND'S STABLE, BUT HE IS IN A COMA.

IN BETWEEN SOBS, **JB** BARELY GETS HIS QUESTION OUT: WILL MY DAD BE HOME FOR CHRISTMAS?

HE LOOKS AT US AND SAYS: TRY TALKING TO HIM, MAYBE HE CAN HEAR YOU, WHICH COULD HELP HIM COME BACK.

WELL, **MAYBE** WE'RE NOT IN A TALKING MOOD, I SAY. JOSHUA BELL, BE RESPECTFUL! MOM TELLS ME.

181

I SHOULDN'T EVEN BE HERE. I SHOULD BE PUTTING ON MY UNIFORM, STRETCHING, GETTING READY TO PLAY IN THE **COUNTY SEMIFINALS.**

BUT INSTEAD, I'M SITTING IN A SMELLY ROOM IN ST. LUKE'S HOSPITAL, LISTENING TO MOM SING "KUMBAYA," WATCHING JORDAN HOLD DAD'S HAND, WONDERING WHY I HAVE TO PUSH WATER UPHILL WITH A RAKE TO TALK TO SOMEONE WHO ISN'T EVEN **LISTENING.**

TO MISS THE **BIGGEST GAME** OF MY **LIFE.**

MY·O·CAR·DI·AL IN·FARC·TION

(MY-OH-CAR-DEE-YUHL IN-FARK-SHUN) NOUN

OCCURS WHEN BLOOD FLOW TO AN AREA OF THE HEART IS BLOCKED FOR A LONG ENOUGH TIME THAT PART OF THE HEART MUSCLE IS **DAMAGED** OR **DIES**.

AS IN: **JB** SAYS THAT HE HATES BASKETBALL BECAUSE IT WAS THE ONE THING THAT DAD LOVED THE MOST BESIDES US AND IT WAS THE ONE THING THAT CAUSED HIS **MYOCARDIAL INFARCTION**.

AS IN: THE DOCTOR SEES ME GOOGLING THE SYMPTOMS—COUGHING, SWEATING, VOMITING, NOSEBLEEDS—AND HE SAYS, YOU KNOW WE CAN'T BE SURE WHAT CAUSES A **MYOCARDIAL INFARCTION**.

I SAY, WHAT ABOUT DOUGHNUTS AND FRIED CHICKEN AND GENETICS?

THE DOCTOR LOOKS AT MY MOM, THEN LEAVES.

AS IN: DAD'S IN A **COMA** BECAUSE OF A **MYOCARDIAL** INFARCTION, WHICH IS THE SAME THING MY **GRANDFATHER** DIED OF.

SO WHAT DOES THAT MEAN FOR ME AND **JB**?

OKAY, DAD

THE DOCTOR SAYS I SHOULD TALK TO YOU, THAT MAYBE YOU CAN HEAR AND MAYBE YOU CAN'T.

MOM AND JB HAVE BEEN TALKING YOUR EAR OFF ALL MORNING.

SO, IF YOU'RE LISTENING, I'D LIKE TO KNOW,
WHEN DID YOU DECIDE TO JUMP SHIP?

I THOUGHT YOU WERE DA MAN.

AND ONE MORE THING:
IF WE MAKE IT TO THE FINALS, I WILL NOT
MISS THE BIG GAME FOR A
SMALL MAYBE.

MOM, SINCE YOU ASKED, I'LL TELL YOU WHY I'M SO ANGRY

BECAUSE DAD TRIED TO DUNK.
BECAUSE I WANT TO WIN A CHAMPIONSHIP.
BECAUSE I CAN'T WIN A CHAMPIONSHIP IF I'M SITTING IN THIS
SMELLY HOSPITAL.

BECAUSE DAD TOLD YOU HE'D BE HERE FOREVER.
BECAUSE I THOUGHT FOREVER WAS LIKE MARS—FAR AWAY.
BECAUSE IT TURNS OUT FOREVER'S LIKE THE MALL—RIGHT AROUND
THE CORNER.

BECAUSE JORDAN DOESN'T TALK BASKETBALL ANYMORE.
BECAUSE JORDAN CUT MY HAIR AND DIDN'T CARE.
BECAUSE HE'S ALWAYS DRINKING SWEET TEA.
BECAUSE SOMETIMES I GET THIRSTY.
BECAUSE I DON'T HAVE ANYBODY TO TALK TO NOW.
BECAUSE I FEEL EMPTY WITH NO HAIR.
BECAUSE CPR DOESN'T WORK!
BECAUSE MY CROSSOVER SHOULD BE BETTER.
BECAUSE IF IT WAS BETTER, THEN DAD WOULDN'T
HAVE HAD THE BALL.

BECAUSE IF DAD HADN'T HAD THE BALL,
THEN HE WOULDN'T HAVE TRIED TO DUNK.

BECAUSE IF DAD HADN'T TRIED TO
DUNK, THEN WE WOULDN'T BE HERE.

BECAUSE I DON'T WANT TO
BE HERE.

BECAUSE THE ONLY THING
THAT MATTERS IS SWISH.

BECAUSE OUR BACKBOARD
IS SPLINTERED.

TEXT MESSAGES FROM VONDIE

8:05
FILTHY, THE GAME WENT DOUBLE OVERTIME
BEFORE THE LAST POSSESSION.

8:05
COACH CALLED A TIME-OUT AND HAD US ALL DO A
SPECIAL CHANT ON THE SIDELINE.

8:06
IT WAS KINDA CREEPY. THE OTHER TEAM WAS **LOL**.
I GUESS IT WORKED, 'CAUSE

8:06
WE WON, **40-39**.
WE DEDICATED THE GAME BALL TO YOUR POP.

8:07
IS HE BETTER? YOU AND **JB** COMING
TO **PRACTICE?**

FILTHY, YOU THERE?

186

ON CHRISTMAS EVE

DAD FINALLY WAKES UP.

HE SMILES AT MOM, HIGH-FIVES JORDAN,
THEN LOOKS RIGHT AT ME AND SAYS,

FILTHY, I DIDN'T JUMP SHIP.

SANTA CLAUS STOPS BY

WE'RE CELEBRATING CHRISTMAS IN DAD'S HOSPITAL ROOM.
FLOWERS AND GIFTS AND CHEER SURROUND HIM.
RELATIVES FROM FIVE STATES.

AUNTS WITH COLLARDS AND YAMS, COUSINS WITH **HOOTS** AND
HOLLERS, AND RUNNY NOSES.

MOM'S SINGING, DAD'S PLAYING SPADES WITH HIS BROTHERS.
I KNOW THE NURSES CAN'T WAIT FOR VISITING HOURS TO END.

I CAN'T EITHER. UNCLE **BOB'S** TURKEY TASTES LIKE CARDBOARD AND
HIS LEMON POUND CAKE LOOKS LIKE **JELL-O**, BUT HOSPITAL SANTA
HAS EVERYONE SINGING AND ALL THIS JOY IS **SPOILING** MY **MOOD**.

I CAN'T REMEMBER THE LAST TIME I SMILED. HAPPY IS A HUGE
RIVER RIGHT NOW AND I'VE FORGOTTEN HOW TO **SWIM**.

AFTER TWO HOURS, MOM TELLS EVERYONE IT'S TIME FOR DAD TO
GET SOME REST. I HUG FOURTEEN PEOPLE, WHICH IS LIKE
DROWNING.

WHEN THEY LEAVE, DAD CALLS JORDAN AND ME OVER TO THE BED.

DO Y'ALL REMEMBER WHEN YOU WERE SEVEN AND JB WANTED TO SWING BUT ALL THE SWINGS WERE FILLED AND FILTHY PUSHED THE LITTLE REDHEAD KID OUT OF THE SWING SO JB COULD TAKE IT?

WELL, IT WASN'T THE RIGHT BEHAVIOR, BUT THE INTENTION WAS RIGHTEOUS.

YOU WERE THERE FOR EACH OTHER.

I WANT YOU BOTH TO ALWAYS BE THERE FOR EACH OTHER.

JORDAN STARTS CRYING.

MOM HOLDS HIM, AND TAKES HIM OUTSIDE FOR A WALK.

ME AND DAD STARE AT EACH OTHER FOR TEN MINUTES WITHOUT SAYING A WORD. I TELL HIM, I DON'T HAVE ANYTHING TO SAY.

FILTHY, SILENCE DOESN'T MEAN WE HAVE RUN OUT OF THINGS TO SAY, ONLY THAT WE ARE TRYING NOT TO SAY THEM.

SO, LET'S DO THIS.

I'LL ASK YOU A QUESTION, THEN YOU ASK ME A QUESTION, AND WE'LL JUST KEEP ASKING UNTIL WE CAN BOTH GET SOME ANSWERS. OKAY?

SURE, I SAY, BUT YOU GO FIRST.

QUESTIONS

HAVE YOU BEEN PRACTICING YOUR FREE THROWS?
WHY DIDN'T YOU GO TO THE DOCTOR WHEN MOM ASKED YOU?

WHEN IS THE GAME?
WHY DIDN'T YOU EVER TAKE US FISHING?

DOES YOUR BROTHER STILL HAVE A GIRLFRIEND?
ARE YOU GOING TO DIE?

DO YOU REALLY WANT TO KNOW?
WHY COULDN'T I SAVE YOU?

DON'T YOU SEE THAT YOU DID?
DO YOU REMEMBER I KEPT PUMPING
AND BREATHING?

AREN'T I ALIVE?
...?

DID Y'ALL ARREST UNCLE BOB'S TURKEY? IT WAS
JUST CRIMINAL WHAT HE DID TO THAT BIRD, WASN'T IT?
YOU THINK THIS IS FUNNY?

HOW'S YOUR BROTHER?
IS OUR FAMILY FALLING APART?

YOU STILL THINK I SHOULD WRITE A BOOK?
WHAT DOES THAT HAVE TO DO WITH
ANYTHING?

WHAT IF I CALL IT "BASKETBALL RULES"?
ARE YOU GOING TO DIE?

DO YOU KNOW I LOVE YOU, SON?
DON'T YOU KNOW THE BIG GAME'S TOMORROW?

IS IT TRUE MOM IS LETTING YOU PLAY?
YOU THINK I SHOULDN'T PLAY?

WHAT DO YOU THINK, FILTHY?
WHAT ABOUT JORDAN?

DOES HE WANT TO PLAY?
DON'T YOU KNOW HE WON'T AS LONG AS YOU'RE IN HERE?

DON'T YOU KNOW I KNOW THAT?
SO, WHY DON'T YOU COME HOME?

CAN'T YOU SEE I CAN'T?
WHY NOT?

DON'T YOU KNOW IT'S COMPLICATED, FILTHY?
WHY CAN'T YOU CALL ME BY MY REAL NAME?

JOSH, DO YOU KNOW WHAT A HEART ATTACK IS?
DON'T YOU REMEMBER I WAS THERE?

DON'T YOU SEE I NEED TO BE HERE SO THEY
CAN FIX THE DAMAGE THAT'S BEEN DONE TO
MY HEART?
WHO'S GONNA FIX THE DAMAGE THAT'S
BEEN DONE TO MINE?

TANKA FOR LANGUAGE ARTS CLASS

THIS CHRISTMAS WAS NOT MERRY, AND I HAVE NOT FOUND JOY IN THE NEW YEAR WITH DAD IN THE HOSPITAL FOR NINETEEN DAYS AND COUNTING.

I DON'T THINK I'LL EVER GET USED TO

WALKING HOME FROM SCHOOL **ALONE**

PLAYING MADDEN **ALONE**

LISTENING TO LIL WAYNE **ALONE**

GOING TO THE LIBRARY **ALONE**

SHOOTING FREE THROWS **ALONE**

WATCHING **ESPN ALONE**

EATING **DOUGHNUTS ALONE**

SAYING MY **PRAYERS ALONE**

NOW THAT **JORDAN'S** IN **LOVE** AND DAD'S LIVING IN A **HOSPITAL**

BASKETBALL RULE #9

WHEN THE GAME IS ON THE LINE,
DON'T FEAR. GRAB THE BALL.

TAKE IT TO THE **HOOP**.

AS WE'RE ABOUT TO LEAVE FOR THE FINAL GAME

THE PHONE RINGS. MOM SHRIEKS.
I THINK THE **WORST**.

I ASK **JB** IF HE HEARD THAT.
HE'S ON HIS BUNK LISTENING TO
HIS iPOD.

MOM RUSHES PAST OUR ROOM,
OUT OF **BREATH**.

JB JUMPS DOWN FROM HIS BUNK.
WHAT'S WRONG, MOM? I ASK.

SHE SAYS:

DAD. HAD. ANOTHER. ATTACK.
NOW. DON'T. WORRY.

I'M. GOING. HOSPITAL.

SEE. YOU. TWO. AT. GAME.

VRUUUUUMMMMMMM

HER CAR **STARTS**.

JB, WHAT SHOULD WE DO? I ASK.

HE'S NO LONGER LISTENING TO **MUSIC**,
BUT HIS **TEARS** ARE LOUD ENOUGH
TO DANCE TO.

HE LACES HIS **SNEAKERS**,
RUNS OUT OF OUR ROOM.

THE GARAGE DOOR OPENS.

I HEAR **FLOP FLOP FLOP**
FROM THE STRAWS ON THE SPOKES
OF HIS BICYCLE WHEELS AS HE FOLLOWS
MOM TO THE HOSPITAL.

I HEAR THE CLOCK:

TICK

TOCK

TICK

TOCK.

I HEAR DAD: YOU SHOULD PLAY IN THE GAME, SON.

A HORN BLOWS.
I HEAR **SLAM SLAM SLAM** AS I SHUT THE DOOR OF VONDIE'S DAD'S CAR.

I HEAR **SCREECH SCREECH SCREECH** AS WE PULL AWAY FROM THE CURB ON OUR WAY TO THE COUNTY CHAMPIONSHIP GAME.

DURING WARM-UPS

I MISS FOUR LAY-UPS IN A ROW, AND COACH HAWKINS SAYS, JOSH, YOU SURE YOU'RE ABLE TO **PLAY**?

IT'S MORE THAN OKAY IF YOU NEED TO GO TO THE HOSPITAL WITH YOUR **FAM—**

COACH, MY DAD IS GOING TO BE **FINE**, I SAY.

PLUS HE WANTS ME TO **PLAY**.

SON, YOU TELLING ME YOU'RE OKAY?

CAN A DEAF PERSON WRITE MUSIC? I ASK COACH.

HE RAISES HIS EYEBROWS, SHAKES HIS HEAD, AND TELLS ME TO GO SIT ON THE BENCH.

I EXCUSE MYSELF TO THE LOCKER ROOM TO CHECK MY CELL PHONE, AND THERE ARE TEXTS FROM MOM.

TEXT MESSAGES FROM MOM, PART TWO

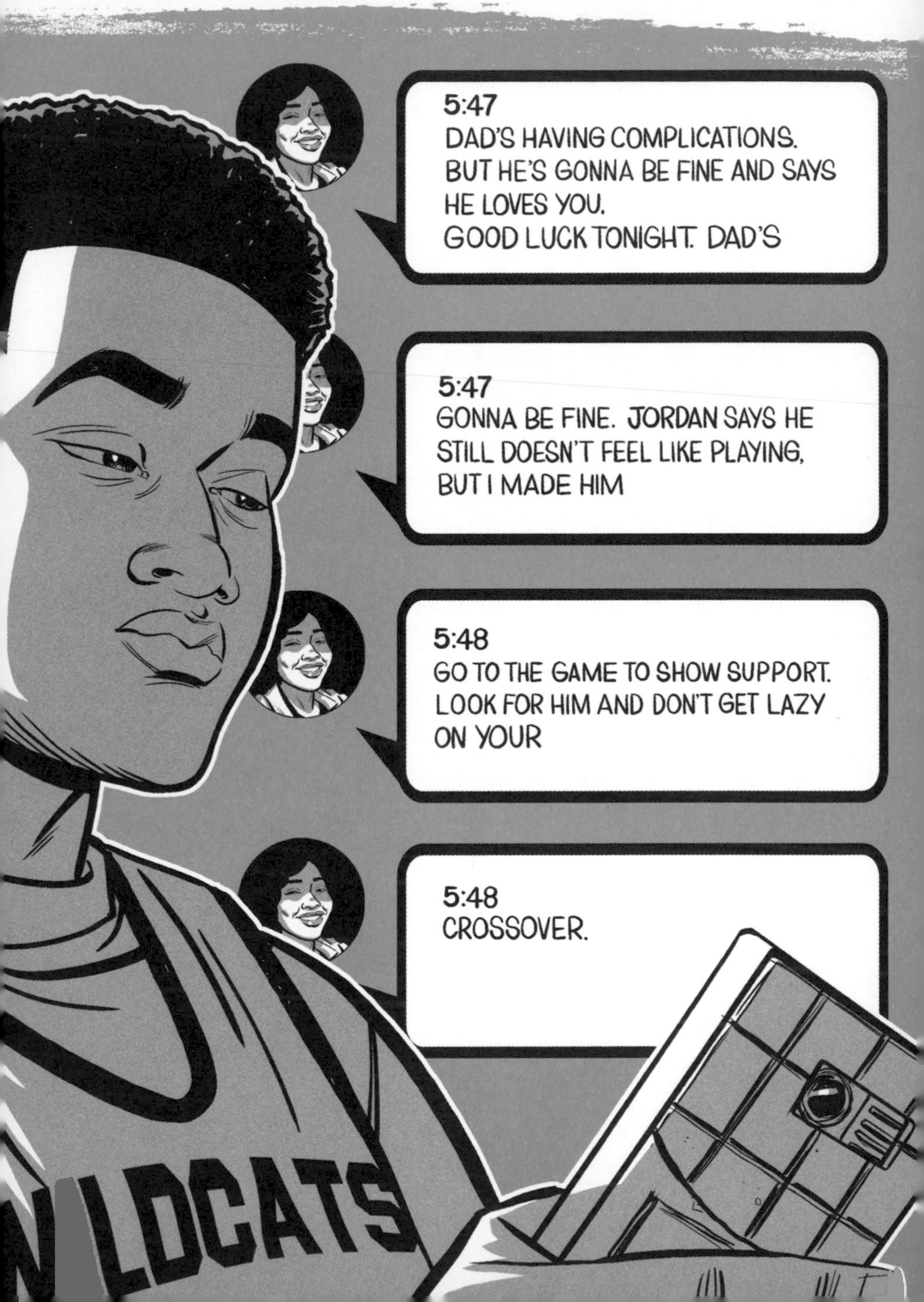

FOR DAD

MY FREE THROW FLIRTS WITH THE RIM AND
LOOPS, TWIRLS, FOR A **MILLION YEARS**,

THEN DROPS, AND FOR ONCE, WE'RE UP, **49–48**,
FIVE DANCERS ON STAGE, LEAPING, JUMPING

SO **HIGH**, SO **FLY**, ELEVEN SECONDS
FROM **SKY**.

A HARD DRIVE, A FAST BREAK,
THEIR BEST PLAYER SLICES THE
THICK AIR TOWARD THE **GOAL**.

HIS PULL-UP JUMPER FLOATS
THROUGH THE **NET**,

THEN EVERYTHING GOES SLOW MOTION:
THE BALL, THE PLAYER . . .

COACH CALLS TIME-OUT
WITH ONLY FIVE SECONDS TO GO.

I WISH THE REF COULD STOP THE CLOCK
OF MY **LIFE**.

JUST ONE MORE GAME.

I THINK MY FATHER IS **DYING**,

AND NOW I AM OUT OF BOUNDS
WHEN I SEE A FAMILIAR FACE
BEHIND OUR BENCH.

MY BROTHER, JORDAN BELL,
HEAD BURIED IN SWEET
TEA, HIS EYES WELLING
WITH HORROR.

BEFORE I KNOW IT, THE WHISTLE BLOWS,
THE BALL IN MY HAND,

THE CLOCK RUNNING DOWN,
MY TEARS RUNNING FASTER.

THE LAST SHOT

5. . . A BOLT OF LIGHTNING ON MY KICKS . . .

THE COURT IS **SIZZLING**

MY SWEAT IS **DRIZZLING**, STOP ALL THAT **QUIVERING**, CUZ TONIGHT I'M DELIVERING, I'M DRIVING DOWN THE LANE, **SLIDING**

4 . . . DRIBBLING TO THE MIDDLE, GLIDING LIKE A BLACK EAGLE. THE CROWD IS **RUMBLING**

RUSTLING **ROARING**

TAKE IT TO THE HOOP.

TAKE IT TO THE HOOP

3 . . . **2** . . . WATCH OUT, 'CUZ I'M ABOUT TO GET **DIRTY** WITH IT, ABOUT TO POUR **FILTHY**'S SAUCE ALL OVER YOU.

OHHHHH, DID YOU SEE McNASTY CROSS OVER YOU? NOW I'M TAKING YOU, ANKLE **BREAKING** YOU, YOU'RE ON YOUR KNEES.

SCREAMIN' **PLEASE, BABY, PLEASE**

1 . . . IT'S A BIRD, IT'S A PLANE.
NO, IT'S **UP UP UPPPPPPPPPP.**

MY SHOT IS **F L O W I N G,**

FLYING,

FLUTTERING

OHHHHHHHH,
THE CHAINS ARE
JINGALING RINGALING AND
SWINGALING
SWISH.

GAME/OVER.

OVERTIME

DAILY NEWS

JANUARY 14

PROFESSIONAL BASKETBALL PLAYER CHARLIE (CHUCK) "DA MAN" BELL COLLAPSED IN A GAME OF ONE-ON-ONE WITH HIS SON JOSH.

AFTER A COMPLICATION, BELL DIED AT ST. LUKE'S HOSPITAL FROM A MASSIVE HEART ATTACK.

ACCORDING TO REPORTS, BELL SUFFERED FROM HYPERTENSION AND HAD THREE FAINTING SPELLS IN THE FOUR MONTHS BEFORE HIS COLLAPSE.

AUTOPSY RESULTS FOUND BELL HAD A LARGE, EXTENSIVELY SCARRED HEART.

REPORTS HAVE SURFACED THAT BELL REFUSED TO SEE A DOCTOR. ONE OF HIS FORMER TEAMMATES STATED, "HE WASN'T A BIG FAN OF DOCTORS AND HOSPITALS, THAT'S FOR SURE."

EARLIER IN HIS LIFE, BELL CHOSE TO END HIS PROMISING BASKETBALL CAREER RATHER THAN HAVE SURGERY ON HIS KNEE.

KNOWN FOR HIS DAZZLING CROSSOVER, CHUCK BELL WAS THE CAPTAIN OF THE ITALIAN TEAM THAT WON BACK-TO-BACK EUROLEAGUE CHAMPIONSHIPS IN THE LATE NINETIES.

HE IS SURVIVED BY HIS WIFE, DR. CRYSTAL STANLEY-BELL, AND HIS TWIN SONS, JOSHUA AND JORDAN, WHO RECENTLY WON THEIR FIRST COUNTY CHAMPIONSHIP.

BELL WAS THIRTY-NINE.

WHERE DO WE GO FROM HERE?

THERE ARE NO COACHES AT FUNERALS.

NO PRACTICE TO GET READY. NO WARM-UP.

THERE IS NO LAST-SECOND SHOT, AND WE ALL WEAR ITS CRUEL MIDNIGHT UNIFORM, STARLESS AND UNFRIENDLY.

I AM UNPREPARED FOR **DEATH**.
THIS IS A GAME I CANNOT PLAY.

IT HAS NO RULES, NO REFEREES.
YOU CANNOT **WIN**.

I LISTEN TO MY FATHER'S TEAMMATES TELL FUNNY STORIES ABOUT LOVE AND BASKETBALL.

I HEAR THE CHOIR'S COMFORT SONGS.

THEY ALMOST DROWN OUT MOM'S **SOBS.**.

SHE WILL NOT LOOK IN THE COFFIN.

THAT IS NOT MY HUSBAND, SHE SAYS.

DAD IS GONE, LIKE THE END OF A GOOD SONG.

WHAT REMAINS IS BONE AND MUSCLE AND COLD SKIN.

I GRAB MOM'S LEFT HAND. JB GRABS HER RIGHT.

THE PREACHER SAYS, A GREAT FATHER, SON, AND HUSBAND HAS
CROSSED OVER. AMEN.

OUTSIDE, A LONG CHARCOAL LIMO PULLS UP TO THE CURB TO
TAKE US BACK.

IF ONLY.

STAR·LESS
(STAHR-LES) ADJECTIVE

WITH NO STARS.

AS IN: IF ME AND JB TRY OUT FOR JV NEXT YEAR, THE REGGIE LEWIS JUNIOR HIGH SCHOOL WILDCATS WILL BE **STARLESS**.

AS IN: LAST NIGHT I FELT LIKE I WAS FADING AWAY AS I WATCHED THE **STARLESS** PORTLAND TRAILBLAZERS GET STOMPED BY DAD'S FAVORITE TEAM, THE LAKERS.

AS IN: MY FATHER WAS THE LIGHT OF MY WORLD, AND NOW THAT HE'S GONE, EACH NIGHT IS **STARLESS**.

BASKETBALL RULE #10

A LOSS IS INEVITABLE, LIKE SNOW IN WINTER. TRUE CHAMPIONS LEARN TO DANCE THROUGH THE STORM.

THERE ARE SO MANY FRIENDS

NEIGHBORS, DAD'S TEAMMATES, AND FAMILY MEMBERS PACKED INTO OUR LIVING ROOM THAT I HAVE TO GO OUTSIDE JUST TO BREATHE.

THE AIR IS FILLED WITH LAUGHTER, JOHN COLTRANE, JAY-Z, AND THE SMELL OF SALMON, PLUS SCENTS OF EVERY PIE AND CAKE IMAGINABLE.

EVEN MOM IS SMILING.
JOSH, DON'T YOU HEAR THE PHONE RINGING?
SHE SAYS.

I DON'T—THE SOUND OF "A LOVE SUPREME"
AND LOUD LAUGHTER DROWNING IT OUT.

CAN YOU GET IT, PLEASE? SHE ASKS ME.

I ANSWER IT, A SALMON SANDWICH
CRAMMED IN MY MOUTH.

HELLO, BELL RESIDENCE,
I MUTTER.

HI, THIS IS ALEXIS.

OH . . . HEY.

I'M SORRY I COULDN'T BE AT
THE **FUNERAL**.

THIS IS JOSH, NOT **JB**.

I KNOW IT'S YOU, **FILTHY.** JB IS **LOUD.**

YOUR PHONE VOICE ALWAYS SOUNDS LIKE IT'S THE BREAK OF DAWN, LIKE YOU'RE JUST WAKING UP, SHE SAYS PLAYFULLY.

I LAUGH FOR THE FIRST TIME IN DAYS. I JUST WANTED TO CALL AND SAY HOW SORRY I AM FOR YOUR LOSS. IF THERE IS ANYTHING MY DAD OR I CAN DO, PLEASE LET US KNOW.

LOOK, ALEXIS, I'M SORRY ABOUT— IT'S ALL GOOD, **FILTHY.** I GOTTA GO, BUT MY SISTER HAS FIVE TICKETS TO SEE **DUKE** PLAY **NORTH CAROLINA.**

ME, HER, **JB,** AND MY DAD ARE GOING. YOU WANNA—

ABSOLUTELY, I SAY, AND **THANKS**, RIGHT BEFORE COACH HAWKINS COMES MY WAY WITH OUTSTRETCHED ARMS AND A BEAR-SIZE HUG, SENDING THE PHONE CRASHING TO THE FLOOR.

ON MY WAY OUT THE DOOR, TO GET SOME FRESH AIR, MOM GIVES ME A KISS AND A PIECE OF SWEET POTATO PIE WITH TWO SCOOPS OF VANILLA SOY ICE CREAM.

WHERE'S YOUR BROTHER? SHE ASKS.

I HAVEN'T SEEN **JB** SINCE THE FUNERAL, BUT IF I HAD TO GUESS, I'D SAY HE'S GOING TO SEE **ALEXIS**.

BECAUSE, IF I HAD A GIRLFRIEND, I'D BE OFF WITH HER RIGHT ABOUT NOW.

BUT I DON'T, SO THE NEXT BEST THING WILL HAVE TO DO.

FREE THROWS

IT ONLY TAKES ME **FOUR** MOUTHFULS
TO FINISH THE DESSERT.

I HAVE TO **JUMP** TO GET THE **BALL**.
IT IS WEDGED BETWEEN RIM AND
BACKBOARD, EVIDENCE OF **JB** TRYING
AND FAILING TO **DUNK**.

I TAP IT OUT AND DRIBBLE
TO THE FREE-THROW LINE.

DAD ONCE MADE FIFTY **FREE THROWS**
IN A **ROW**.

THE MOST I EVER MADE WAS
NINETEEN.

I GRIP THE BALL, PLANT MY FEET ON
THE LINE, AND SHOOT THE FIRST ONE.

IT GOES IN.

I LOOK AROUND TO SEE IF ANYONE IS
WATCHING.

NOPE. NOT ANYMORE.

THE NEXT TWELVE SHOTS ARE GOOD.

I NAME THEM EACH A YEAR IN MY LIFE.
A YEAR WITH MY FATHER.

BY TWENTY-SEVEN, I AM MAKING THEM WITH MY EYES CLOSED.
THE ORANGE ORB HAS WINGS LIKE THERE'S AN ANGEL TAKING IT
TO THE HOOP.

ON THE FORTY-NINTH SHOT, I AM ONLY SLIGHTLY AWARE THAT I
AM MOMENTS FROM FIFTY.

THE ONLY THING THAT REALLY MATTERS IS THAT OUT HERE IN THE
DRIVEWAY SHOOTING FREE THROWS I FEEL CLOSER TO DAD.

YOU FEEL BETTER? HE ASKS.

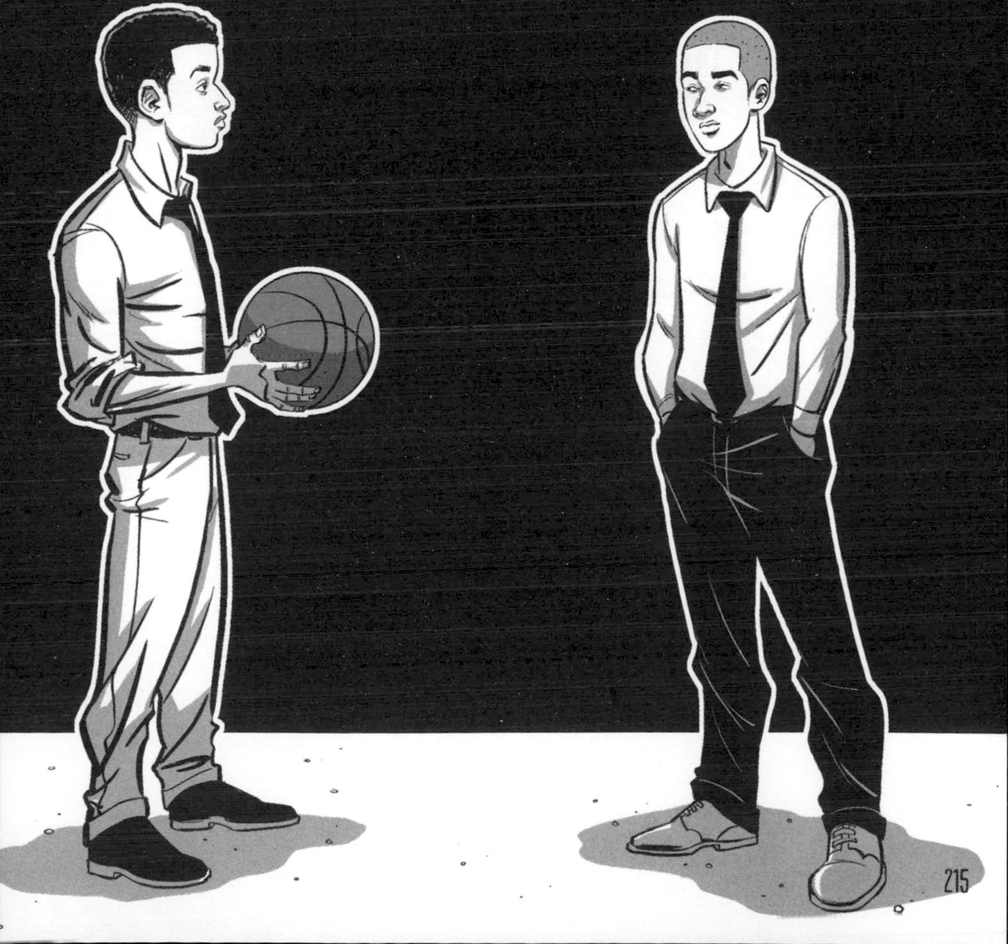

DID YOU TALK TO DAD BEFORE—

HE TOLD US TO STAY OUT OF HIS CLOSET.

THEN HE TOLD ME TO GIVE YOU THIS.

YOU EARNED IT, **FILTHY**, HE SAYS, SLIDING THE RING ON MY FINGER.

MY HEART LEAPS INTO MY THROAT.

DAD'S CHAMPIONSHIP RING. BETWEEN THE BOUNCING AND SOBBING, I WHISPER, **WHY?**

I GUESS YOU **DA MAN** NOW, FILTHY, JB SAYS. AND FOR THE FIRST TIME IN MY LIFE I DON'T WANT TO BE.

I BET THE DISHES YOU MISS **NUMBER FIFTY**, HE SAYS, WALKING AWAY.

WHERE'S HE GOING?

HEY, I SHOUT.

WE **DA MAN**.

AND WHEN HE TURNS AROUND I TOSS HIM THE **BALL**.

HE DRIBBLES BACK TO THE TOP OF THE KEY, FIXES HIS EYES ON THE GOAL.

I WATCH THE BALL LEAVE HIS HANDS LIKE A **BIRD**

UP **HIGH**, SKATING THE SKY, CROSSING OVER US.